About the Author

Zachary Smith wrote his first book at age ten. He is an avid horror and science fiction fan. *Danny and the Forbidden Devils* is the first in the Danny series and Zach's debut.

Danny and the Forbidden Devils

Zachary Smith

Danny and the Forbidden Devils

Olympia Publishers
London

www.olympiapublishers.com
OLYMPIA PAPERBACK EDITION

A CIP catalogue record for this title is
available from the British Library.

ISBN: 978-1-78830-618-8

First Published in 2020

Olympia Publishers
Tallis House
2 Tallis Street
London
EC4Y 0AB
Printed in Great Britain

Danny

Danny stopped at the end of the hall and waited. The flunky he was chasing had a revolver and he had already fired it three times, meaning he had three shots left. Danny kicked a paint can over and caused the flunky to fire two more rounds, and then he aimed his pistol and shot twice clipping the guy in the arm with one. All this had gone south when Neil, Danny's partner, had lost his cool and gotten himself shot and now Danny was left to clean the shit show up.

The guy took off down the hall leaving a clear trail behind him as Danny followed. They exited into a large room where the drugs were produced and packaged. Danny dropped and rolled to avoid the guy's last shot then popped up only to be hit with a slug in the chest. Danny fell back, the hole in his chest gushing blood as he tried to figure out how he had miscounted.

He could feel the power inside him welling up, fighting its way to the surface. He had tried for so long to keep it buried, keep it from ever seeing the light of day again but yet here he was, lying on the floor bleeding out and his only means of surviving this was to let the beast take control. Danny closed his eyes, feeling it clawing its way forward like some caged animal. He opened his eyes with a scream that turned to a roar, the hole in his chest beginning to close as his eyes turned a bright red. A smokey haze surrounded him as he got to his feet.

As he steadied himself, the smokey haze slowly took shape into two large snake-like appendages. The snakes opened their mouths which were covered by four taloned appendages; the mouths underneath, were lined with razor-sharp teeth. The flunky began to reload his gun.

"What the fuck are you?"

"The devil," Danny said, before extending his hands forward.

The snakes shot forward towards the guy, grabbing him by his left arm and right leg. They raised him into the air then pulled in opposite directions, tearing his limbs from his body. Each snake swallowed the limb they had torn free then returned to Danny, slowly dissipating into the hazy smoke from which they appeared.

Tyler

Tyler entered the bar; had anyone been paying any attention to him, they would have noticed how jumpy he was. He walked up to the bar and laid some money down.

"Anything is fine."

The bartender took the money then threw together a quick drink and slid it over to Tyler. Tyler took a sip from his drink then headed for the back of the bar to find Danny. He couldn't deny he was a man in need of help; hell, the info he had put a pretty high price on his head and the only person he trusted now was Danny. Thousands of demons he knew and the only one he trusted was the same one that tried to kill him several years earlier — irony, right? Tyler slid into the booth, without waiting for Danny to ask him to sit, and took another sip of his drink.

"I'm safe in assuming you're in trouble?" Danny said, without looking up from the newspaper laid out on the table.

"You haven't even looked at me, how could you know?"

"One, the way you entered the bar — a deaf cave demon could have heard you. Two, you're frazzled, jittery. Your eyes keep looking to the door. Three, your shirt is on inside out. Shall I keep going, or do you want to just skip to the part where you tell me what's going on?"

"Will you look at me?" Tyler said, grabbing the paper and throwing it on the floor.

Danny sighed and sat back in the booth looking at Tyler. Danny motioned for Tyler to begin.

"Sorry, but I need your help. I'm in it deep this time, Danny. I head and saw some shit I wasn't meant to. They killed Lilly; I escaped before they found me, but I think they know I was there."

"And you can't handle this on your own?"

"This is the part you are going to love," Tyler said, before taking a sip of his drink. "Oswald Sheppard was there."

The name had indeed got Danny's attention. Danny sighed sitting forward then leaning out of the booth and picking up the paper.

"Sorry, but I can't help you. Go find Bruce or Logan, maybe they will help you."

"Danny, you're the only person I trust. I know about your history with the Sheppards..."

"No. People think they know. They've heard stories, but no one really knows what went on behind those walls."

"Which is why you should help me. We can destroy them. You, personally, know the fucked-up shit that they do, and I know what I heard last night. Let's bring them down."

Danny was quiet for a moment, thinking over his options. He didn't want to get involved with the Sheppards again, but if they were working on the same stuff they were, when Danny had been there, he knew they had to be stopped.

"What did you hear?"

"A virus. Lilly had seen first-hand what the virus was capable of and she was going to expose them. Lilly was one of their lab technicians and a friend of mine. She called it a doomsday virus. She didn't get to tell me much before Oswald and his goons showed up. I was seen there that night and many nights before that so it's only a matter of time before they get to me."

Danny folded the paper up and slid it across the table to Tyler. Tyler looked down at the paper and the article it was folded to; the article was titled 'Rage Demon Trashes Supermarket'.

"We're gonna need some friends, a lot of them," Danny said, with a smile.

Oswald

Valentine, Oswald's assistant, knocked and entered his office. Oswald turned to face the woman as she entered.

"You have a visitor, sir."

"Get him out of here," Oswald said, to the two men standing behind him.

The two men grabbed up the man off the floor and dragged him out of the room, while a third man began wiping the blood from the floor. Oswald sat down behind his desk and motioned for Valentine to let in his visitor. Valentine opened the door and a beautiful woman entered.

"Dana Chadwick. To what do I owe the pleasure?"

"I see Daddy is trusting you in his absence to run things here. Feels good, doesn't it? All that power that comes with the Sheppard name."

"Come on, Dana, I know you. You didn't come here to talk politics. You came to see if you could shake down the new young Sheppard, get him under your thumb."

"You know me too well, Oswald," she said, sitting down in front of the desk. "The witches' coven wants an alliance with the Sheppard Empire."

"That may not sit well with others. I have the warlocks by my side already."

"Who refuses to join your cause? The Demons. The witches' coven has deep reaches into the demon ranks, and we can work them, bring them to your side."

"I'll need something, let's call it a means to earn trust, a demon that goes by the name Tyler Bogart. Bring him to me, alive, and we'll work on an alliance."

"Consider it done."

Bruce

Danny and Tyler sat down in the small square room and waited while a guard went to retrieve Bruce Holland, the rage demon. Tyler looked around the small room, glad this was as close to being locked up as he had ever been. He didn't think he could handle being locked up like some kind of animal.

"What makes you think he's just going to join us all willy nilly?" Tyler asked, looking over at Danny.

"Demons become desperate once they have been locked up for a while."

"He's been locked up for eight hours. Eight hours."

"It's enough for someone like him. Trust me."

The door on the other side of the table opened and a guy with light brown hair, black eyeliner, and black fingernails, who Tyler guessed was Bruce was led in then cuffed to the table. Tyler wondered if Danny had been wrong, this guy didn't look on the edge of breaking, he looked fine. Tyler looked over at Danny who was still sitting quietly as the guard left. The silence lasted a minute longer then Bruce began to speak and Tyler saw Danny had been right.

"You have to get me out of here. I'm going fuckin' looney in here. I've been here what... two years?" Bruce's hyper attitude faded as Danny's silence remained. "Four years?"

Danny looked over at Tyler with a smile then leaned forward resting his arms on the table.

"Bruce, you have been here for eight hours."

"Oh God," Bruce said, and covered his face. "I'm going to end up offing myself in here."

"You don't have to. My friend and I came with an option. We could use..."

"I'm in."

"You don't want me to finish explaining?"

"I don't care what you want me to do as long as it gets me out of here."

"Well, Bruce, welcome to our ragtag team." Danny stood and turned to Tyler. "One down, six to go. Stay here while I go find out how much it's gonna cost me to get him out of here."

"Wait. You're going to leave me in here by myself with him?" Tyler asked, as Danny closed the door behind him.

Tyler turned back around to face Bruce who was sitting at the table with his head resting on his hands. Tyler couldn't put his finger on it, but something about Bruce made him uncomfortable — maybe it was because rage demons were known for blowing up over the smallest things.

"Sup?" Bruce said, with a smile that let Tyler know he knew he was unnerving him.

Megan

Megan leaned against the wall next to the door as several people walked by then, once clear, she climbed up the side of the building until she reached a window on the fourth floor. She pushed the window open and dropped down inside the apartment. The room was dark, only faintly lit by a small desk lamp on the desk in the back of the room.

Megan walked back to the desk and began looking through the papers on it, though unable to find what she was looking for. She opened the drawers and sifted through the files in them before closing them and sighing. She walked over to the door and opened it slightly; she didn't hear anything. She pulled the door open and stepped out into the hall and slowly made her way down the hall.

She opened the door to her right and stepped inside. This room was dark, no lights at all. She felt around for a switch but, before she found one, a lamp turned on across the room. Sitting in a chair by the lamp was a woman cradling a folder and black velvet sack sat on top of it.

"Looking for this?"

"You know I am. So why play dumb?"

"You honestly thought I wouldn't think you would come for it? I saw your face when I won the bidding. Tell me one thing: why is it so important to you?"

"Big ruby, big payoff."

"Please, if it were simply a matter of a payoff, you wouldn't have been willing to drop nearly two million on it."

"My client offered me double upon delivery."

"Your client. Damn Sheppards have their fingers in everything."

"Give me the ruby," Megan said, stepping closer.

"I know how these things work. You are to kill me, but let me give you a little dirt on your precious client," the woman said, and tossed the file onto the floor at Megan's feet. "Read it and decide for yourself if this is who you really want to be working for."

"The ruby," Megan said, holding her hand out.

The woman handed Megan the velvet bag then laid her hands in her lap. She knew she would be dead in a few minutes and she was ready to accept her fate, she just hoped the girl robbing her would read what was in the file.

"Get it over with," the woman said.

Megan pulled a pistol from her thigh holster and aimed at the woman's chest. A faint feeling of guilt caressed Megan before she pulled the trigger, then nothing. Megan holstered her gun then picked up the file off the floor.

Danny

They had traveled about two hours before Danny pulled the truck over at a Chinese buffet restaurant and put it in park. Tyler looked around, trying to figure out why they were stopping.

"What are we doing?" Tyler asked.

"It's lunchtime," Danny said, getting out of the truck. "And our next recruit is in here."

"I could go for some Chinese," Bruce said, climbing out of the back of the truck.

They walked up to the ornately carved red doors and pulled them open. The inside was even more striking than the outside. A golden dragon was carved into the ceiling and the walls were adorned with all sorts of paintings and other Chinese decorations.

"So who are we meeting in a buffet?" Bruce asked.

"A glutton demon," Tyler answered before Danny could.

"How much can you eat?" Danny asked, squeezing Tyler's shoulder.

"If you're asking me if I want to try and out eat a glutton demon, no."

"Bruce?"

"I... I have a very sensitive digestive track so..."

"Alright. Here," Danny said, handing Tyler the truck keys. "This is gonna hurt."

"Can't we just beat the shit out of him until he agrees to join?" Bruce asked.

"You've never met a glutton demon before have you? They are very tough, and loyal to a fault once you have earned their respect. I don't have to out eat him, I just have to eat enough that he respects my effort as a non-glutton."

They walked back to the back of the restaurant where there was an Asian guy sitting in a booth with a table covered in food and surrounded by several girls. Tyler was surprised when he saw the guy, he had been expecting a fat guy but the guy sitting at the booth was buff.

"Let me do the talking. Johnny can be a little... short-fused."

"I gotta say I was expecting a huge fat guy not someone who looks like they could kick my ass blindfolded," Bruce said, as they approached the table.

"Johnny Yang," Danny said.

Johnny set his empty glass down and belched. As soon as his glass hit the table, the girl to his right was there to fill it back up, while the girl on his left made sure he never ran out of food.

"Who are you? What do you want?" Johnny asked.

"I'm Danny; these are my friends Tyler and Bruce. We were hoping to get you to join our cause. The Sheppards, you've heard of them no doubt."

"I have."

"The things they are working on... we've got to put an end to it. Tyler here overhead and saw somethings and they will no doubt be after him before long. He told me everything he head and saw and along with my history with the Sheppards; I'm shutting them down, but I'm going to need help."

"If anyone hates the Sheppards as much as I do, I will gladly join their cause. I'll help."

Danny gave a silent sigh of relief, but it was too soon.

"But. Let's see how much you can eat."

Danny pulled the chair in front of him out and sat down and took a couple of deep breaths.

"Leelee, hook my new friend here up with the Johnny special."

The girl named Leelee left to gather food while the other set a glass down and filled it with the same amber liquid Johnny was drinking. Leelee returned with two plates piled high with food. Danny looked at the mounds of food and swallowed his dread and dug in.

"If you can clean six plates, you'll have my respect," Johnny said, watching Danny eat.

"I'm gonna go over here cause he's gonna vomit and if I see him vomit, I'm going to vomit," Bruce said, heading for a booth a little way away.

Danny had managed four plates and they were instantly replaced by Leelee as soon as they were empty. Danny sat back in his chair and rubbed his bloated belly and tried to keep from puking.

"Wanna give up?" Johnny asked, with a smirk.

"You got this," Tyler said, massaging Danny's shoulders.

Danny thought he was surely about to spew all the food he had eaten. Danny pushed the plate away and sat back again.

"I'm done," Danny said, putting his fist to his mouth.

"You doubled my expectations," Johnny said, sticking his hand out to Danny.

Danny shook Johnny's hand then they both stood up. Danny's bloated belly could plainly be seen through his tight black tee. Johnny reached over and patted Danny's belly.

"You pregnant?" Johnny laughed. "Go upstairs. You all can stay here tonight, food coma is gonna hit you in a minute. We'll head out in the morning."

Johnny led Danny, Tyler, and Bruce upstairs and to their room. Bruce abandoned them for the sauna with Johnny, while Danny and Tyler retired to the room. Tyler sat down on one of the beds and turned on the TV and began flipping through the stations while Danny pulled off his shirt and fell back onto the other bed.

"Anything you want to watch?" Tyler asked.

"No. I'm sleeping," Danny said, unbuttoning his pants to give his distended belly a little more room.

After a while, Bruce came back and plopped down in a chair and looked around the room taking the scene in. After a minute of uncomfortable staring, Bruce finally spoke.

"You don't have a shirt on; he doesn't have a shirt on and his pants are unbuttoned...What the fuck has been going on in here?"

"I sleep like this. He was in the middle of changing and passed out. Nothing like what your dirty mind is concocting happened."

"I believe you. I have this crazy desire to just poke his stomach."

"Let him rest. We need to rest too; we got an early start in the morning."

Bruce stood up and looked around the room.

"So how is the bed situation gonna work? I don't mind sharing; just keep your man parts that way and I'll keep mine this way."

"That won't be a problem," Tyler said, grabbing an extra pillow off Danny's bed and putting it between himself and Bruce.

"Good night, sweet'ums," Bruce said.

"Is it your personal mission in life to make me as uncomfortable as possible?"

"If it works," Bruce laughed.

Logan

Rain poured down on the city as Logan scoped out the deal going down by the docks. He had been trailing the guy who had the product up for sale tonight, and he was surprised when he saw who the guy was selling to, Oswald Sheppard. Logan dropped to the street below and walked up to the gates leading to the docks; there were seven guards in this area. He knew he could easily take them on; it was the guy with Sheppard he was worried about.

Sheppard's right-hand man, Butch would be the problem. Butch didn't look like much but Logan had tangoed with him before and nearly didn't make it out. Logan pulled two daggers from his chest harness and started forward.

"Bonjour," Logan said, getting the guards attention. "Je suis ici pour te botter le cul."

Logan slit the closest guards throat then spun and threw the daggers taking out two more. He grabbed two more daggers and threw them taking down two more leaving two guards to deal with. He dodged their blows and used another dagger to slice one guard across the gut then spun and brought the blade up into the last guard's chin.

"Repose en paix," he said, and retrieved his daggers and slid them back into his chest harness and made his way further in.

Logan stopped behind a storage container and listened as the men talked. He glanced around trying to figure out his next move. He wasn't looking to take on Sheppard or Butch, he just wanted to grab the product and flee. He had to figure out what a Sheppard was doing in France. He counted four guards along with Butch; he had to act quickly before they realized half their men were dead. Logan started to make his move when gunshots broke the silence and hit the container above his head.

Logan ducked and rolled pulling two daggers from his harness and flung them at his attackers and turned to change his pursuit to Sheppard but had a fist collide with his forehead. His vision went red then black. Logan fell to the ground unconscious and Butch put a foot on his head.

"Want me to squash him, boss?"

"No. He may come in handy later. Demons are like the stray dogs of us cryptids. Turn him over," Oswald said, retrieving a silver case from his car. "Dogs can be trained. We just need to tag our dog so he's easier to find."

Butch rolled Logan over onto his back while Oswald opened the case and removed the gun-shaped device. Oswald walked over to Logan and knelt down beside him, he pushed Logan's shirt up and placed the tip of the gun about four inches to the right of Logan's bellybutton and pulled the trigger. There was a click and when he removed the gun there was a small amount of blood and a small cut.

"Now our dog is tagged," Oswald said, putting the gun away and showing Butch the screen on the inside top of the case.

"What about what he saw or heard?" Butch asked.

"Clean up the dead guards then give him a healthy dose of this," Oswald said, handing Butch a syringe.

"What's this?"

"Personal concoction. Trust me, he'll fail any drug test and lose any credibility to what he says. Once you get the area clean, give the cops an anonymous tip about a tweaker out on the docks."

Oswald put the case back in the car and picked up a pistol from the seat and turned back to his seller.

"Thank you for your help," Oswald said, then shot the man in the head, and then turned back to Butch. "Don't take too long, we have much to do."

Butch nodded as Oswald got in his car and pulled off. Butch felt around on Logan's arm for a vein then stuck the needle in and injected Oswald's drug then began cleaning up the bodies that now littered the docks.

Danny

Danny woke up to find himself alone in their room. He sat up on the edge of the bed and rubbed his eyes sighing. He pulled his phone out of his pocket and looked at the time, at half-past ten. The bathroom door opened and Bruce walked out with a towel wrapped around his waist.

"Good morning, sleeping beauty. How was your food coma?"

"I may never eat Chinese food again."

"You say that now," Bruce said, walking over to a stack of clothes. "Tyler and the Asian guy went and got some supplies. You have some new clothes over there."

"All right. Thanks."

"I'm bi-sexual so I don't care if you see me naked, but if you don't want to, you need to look that way or you're gonna see these sexy little ass cheeks."

"Keep yourself covered. I'm gonna get my clothes and go into the bathroom," Danny said, getting up and walking over to the stack of cloths on the TV cabinet. "Where are they now?"

"Last time I saw them the Asian guy, he was teaching Tyler how to use a sword."

Danny took his clothes into the bathroom and got

dressed. He then headed out into the hall to try and find Tyler and Johnny. He made his way down the hall and into the room on the left where Johnny was showing Tyler how to use a Katana.

"Up and step back with your away foot. Good. Now strike."

Danny leaned up against the doorframe and watched Tyler mirror the moves Johnny was showing him and thought back to the first time he had met Tyler, they had both been so young back then. Tyler, like always, was in trouble and Danny stepped in. That had been before Danny had gotten sucked into the Sheppard's empire, and had been altered. They had unlocked something deep within him that he had never knew existed, a darkness that constantly fought to be free.

"Danny."

Danny was pulled out of his memories by Tyler calling his name. Danny shook off the memories and stepped into the room.

"Yea."

"Want to learn how to use it?" Tyler asked, holding the sword out.

"Nah, I'm good. Thanks."

"You know how to use one," Johnny said, tossing a sword to Danny. "Show me what you got."

Danny caught the sword and unsheathed it as Johnny took the sword from Tyler and readied himself for Danny's attack. Danny lunged first, but Johnny easily blocked his swing and sidestepped with a smile.

"You prefer guns. But some situations can't be handled with guns," Johnny said, attacking several times. "A blade may be your only option."

Johnny swung several more times and Danny blocked and dodged each blow with ease. After another few minutes of swinging and dodging, Johnny tossed his sword to the floor and raised his fists.

"And other times you may have to rely on just your hands. How's your hand to hand combat?"

"Better than you think," Danny said, tossing his sword and readying for Johnny's swings.

Danny and Johnny began their fight as Bruce walked in and stopped beside Tyler. Bruce was surprised to see the two of them going at each other.

"Is this something we should get involved in, or are they just screwing around?" Bruce asked.

"Screwing around, I hope. I think he's just trying to see how much Danny knows when it comes to fighting."

"Asians are martial arts masters. And math."

The two of them seemed to be equally matched, neither had managed to land a hit on each other until Johnny brought his foot up and connected it with the side of Danny's head. Danny went down to his knees, he felt the lump coming up over his right eye then shook his head trying to clear his vision.

"What the hell? You said, hand to hand combat."

"Never trust your opponent to play by the rules," Johnny said, and offered Danny a hand. "Go again?"

"I'm gonna kick your ass this time," Danny said, as Johnny pulled him to his feet.

"We'll see," Johnny said, using the hand he was holding to flip Danny and lay him out on his back.

Danny groaned as the wind was knocked out of him.

Johnny took a couple of steps back as Danny stumbled to his feet and lifted his fists again. Johnny laughed then was on Danny again before Danny had time to react. Johnny connected several punches to Danny's stomach then one to Danny's chin which put Danny back on his back. Danny glared at Johnny who was ready for another attack.

"There it is," Johnny said, noticing the faint red around Danny's irises. "Get mad, let that darkness take control."

Danny laid there a moment fighting to keep the beast inside him contained, it wanted so desperately to be free, to tear Johnny limb from limb and feast on his flesh. Danny closed his eyes and took a deep breath then opened his eyes and got to his feet.

"I'm done," Danny said, heading for the door.

Johnny grabbed one of the swords from the floor and threw it like a javelin into Danny's back. Danny looked down at the tip of the sword protruding from his chest and the red began coming back. He looked back over his shoulder at Johnny who was smiling and the red intensified.

"I want to see it," Johnny said.

A faint wind rustled the posters hanging on the walls and the overhead lights dimmed and flickered as Danny's darkness emerged. Danny turned to face Johnny as the two snake-like appendages appeared over his shoulders. Danny extended his left hand towards Johnny and the snake on the left shot forward. Johnny dodged the first attack, but Danny had sent the second one while Johnny was dodging the first. The second snake bit into Johnny's arm and slung him through the air and into the far wall.

Danny thrust his arms out again sending both snakes onto Johnny— one grabbing his left arm and the other his side, and lifted him up into the air.

"Danny!" Tyler said, grabbing Danny's arm and shaking him. "Danny, stop!"

"Move," Bruce said, pushing Tyler out of the way then smacking Danny hard across the cheek. Danny slowly turned his head towards Bruce. "Oh shit."

Danny grabbed Bruce by the throat and lifted him off the floor.

"Flare... cabinet beside you," Johnny said.

Tyler flung open the doors and dug through the array of objects until he found the flare. He pulled off the cap and struck it. The bright flash of light made the snake-like creatures drop Johnny and flee back to Danny who in turn dropped Bruce. Tyler held the flare out towards the snake creatures and took a step towards Danny. As Tyler drew closer to Danny the snakes began to diminish and the red around Danny's eyes faded. The smokey gray material of the snakes evaporated into Danny's back then Danny let out a sigh and fell forward.

"The fuck was that?" Bruce asked, breathlessly.

"The stories are true, and I'm sad to say he has no control over the darkness within him."

"Shit. Do I need to call an ambulance?" Tyler said, noticing the gushing wound on Johnny's side.

"Just a flesh wound. Grab Leelee, she has stitched me up more times than I can count. He'll need some too," Johnny nodded to Danny passed out on the floor the sword still going through him.

"You know all this is your fault right. You were the one who had to shish kabob him and piss him off, and I thought I was the rage demon."

"I had to see if he really had it. We have to help him control it so he doesn't lose control like that again."

"Has what?"

"Archdemon blood," Johnny replied. "You ever wondered why he hates the Sheppards so much? The shit they did to him, which included infusing him with archdemon blood. Who knows what his limits are? I mean, I threw a fuckin' sword through him and it didn't slow him down in the least."

Bruce looked over at Danny passed out on the floor and got a strange feeling of empathy and dread. He felt bad for Danny yet something told him he was in for one hell of a ride.

Dana

Dana returned to the witches' coven after her meeting with Oswald, she had accomplished what she had set out to, gained the trust of the family that would soon rule the new world. She Had everything in place for the coming storm, Oswald thought the witches and Warlocks were at each other's throats yet the two covens were working together to steak their claim in the new world.

Dana entered the mess hall where the covens had gathered to feast in celebration of their new alliance, although Dana had other plans for their 'alliance'. Dana walked to the front of the room to the head table where her right and left hand sat along with the three warlock leaders. Dana took her seat beside Taka, the warlock head, and nodded her hello.

"Glad you could join us. I take it the meeting with Oswald went as planned."

"We wouldn't be having this conversation if it hadn't. I trust my ladies have accommodated all of your men's needs?"

"Very much so," Taka said, looking about the room of witches and warlocks before them. "A war with the Sheppards isn't going to be an easy one; you sure you want to go through with this?"

"Taka Ikuta, you're not backing out on me, are you?"

"Never. A war with the Sheppards is something we have wanted for a very long time. Having allies in this war is the only thing that has held us back."

"To the fall of the Sheppards," Dana said, raising her glass then taking a sip.

She almost felt bad for Taka. He had no idea what he had gotten himself and his entire coven into by coming here tonight. His whole coven would end here tonight with only the exception of himself and the other two coven heads, Judah and Michael. Dana leaned forward and looked past Taka to Michael. He was leaned back in his chair; his shirt was unbuttoned while one of Dana's witches rubbed his chest while kissing him. The charms had worked perfectly on him, Judah hadn't even required a spell, and all it took to get him numb to the events around him was a bottomless supply of alcohol.

Dana would make her move soon. Her witches would slaughter every warlock and she could mold the remaining warlock head to her will. She looked over at Judah beside Taka, he had lost his shirt sometime while she had been gone to her meeting with Sheppard and had seven empty beer mugs in front of him. One of Dana's witches was standing behind him, kissing his back and neck as he chugged down the remained of his eighth mug.

"Taka. Tell me, with us witches we're all like family; is it the same with your coven?"

"With these two, yeah," Taka said, motioning towards Judah and Michael. "With the others, it's more of a leader and soldier's type relationship."

"Interesting," Dana said, then pulled a dagger from inside her sleeve and placed it to Taka's throat.

"What are you doing Dana?"

"Making sure things go smoothly."

There was a yell and Taka looked up to see several of his men clutching their throats as blood oozed through their fingers. He went to move but Dana pressed the blade harder against his neck.

"Don't move."

Taka looked over at Judah and Michael who seemed oblivious to what was happening.

"Don't worry, they are as safe as you are. But no more aware of what is unfolding than a gazelle being hunted by a lion. Michael is under a seduction spell and, hell, a spell wasn't even necessary for little Judah. All I needed was lots of drink but, to be sure, we put him under a mild seduction spell."

Taka watched as his men were slaughtered before him, each one having their throat slit. The stone floor of the mess hall was splattered by blood and pools formed from all the bodies laid around the room.

"So is this Oswald's plan?"

"No. I meant what I said. I want us to work together to bring Oswald down. I've grown to trust you Taka, but with that kind of army behind you, it was putting a damper on our trust. Now with just the three of you, I can trust you and we can accomplish so much more."

Dana removed the blade from Taka's neck and slid it back into her sleeve.

"Now, we can move forward," she said, offering Taka her hand.

"You expect me to leave my only remaining warlocks here alone with your people?"

"Taka. I would never hurt your brother," she said, rubbing Judah's right shoulder. "Or your best friend. I need the three of you."

Taka hesitated a moment then stood up. "What's next?"

Devon

Devon had kicked back in his new office, his feet propped up on the desk as he looked around at all the stuff his father had left behind. He would have to get rid of most of his old man's stuff to liven up the place, as it was it was about as much fun as a morgue. He had already attacked the bar, there were several bottles strewn across the desk where he had tried several drinks. The large windows behind him cast brilliant rays of sunlight into the office with its dark wood walls. Twenty years old and he was now the runner of one of the world's largest pharmaceutical companies in the world, most people just saw him as some emo, punk rock guy.

He spun around to look out the window and the cityscape outside; thirty stories up really put the city into perspective. The cars and people below all looked so tiny and Devon felt like a king overlooking his kingdom.

"Mr. Mileski," Masato said, entering the room. "Are you finding everything to your liking?"

"Mr. Mileski. Masato you're like five years older than me, we have known each other our whole lives. Call me Devon. Mr. Mileski makes me sound old and responsible."

"Sorry," Masato said, with a bow.

"Is that get up comfortable?" Devon asked, walking over

to Masato and feeling the material. "No bullshit."

"It's... manageable."

"Big changes are coming, Masato. You and I are gonna go places. Dress comfortably tomorrow, t-shirt and jeans, or whatever you find comfortable," Devon said, walking over to the bar. "My dad started something great here, but he was too afraid to expand on his ideas. That's where you and I come in. Did you know, there is a whole weapon research lab about thirty-two stories below our feet?"

"I wasn't aware of that, sir."

"My father was working on something years back. A project that got mothballed five years ago," Devon said, pouring two glasses. "My father, along with three others, were working on this same project until it was deemed too unpredictable."

"And what was this project they were working on?"

"A cure-all," Devon said, handing Masato one of the glasses. "A virus to cure every ailment known to man. Everything."

"If it was a pharmaceutical endeavor, why was it being researched in a weapons lab?"

"If you can cure all, you can also cause all. The perfect weapon: silent and undetectable. We're going to un-mothball it. We're going to pursue a cure-all."

"And the reverse?"

"I'm not interested in weapons. This project was about my mother, I know it. My father abandoned it after she passed and after he figured out it could be used as a weapon. I want to eradicate cancer so no other child has to go through what I did in watching my mother suffer."

"Noble. But how do you keep evil hands from getting

hold and using it as a weapon? There's always a devil lurking in every shadow."

"That's the question," Devon said, leaning back against the desk.

The phone on the desk buzzed and Devon hit the speaker button and waited on the receptionist to speak.

"Mr. Mileski, Oswald Sheppard is on his way up."

"Shit," Devon said, standing up and looking around the office. "Can you clean these bottles up?"

Masato quickly set about picking up the bottles and returning them to the bar while Devon picked up books and papers he had strewn across the desk and floor. The last thing he wanted was for Sheppard to find out about his father's secret project. He may have to deal with Oswald occasionally but he in no way considered him a friend or even trustworthy.

"Your glass," Masato said, motioning to the glass in Devon's hand.

Devon had forgotten all about the drink he had poured or that it was even in his hand. He turned it up and emptied it then handed it to Masato.

"Ready?"

"Would it matter if I said, no? I mean this is your devil in the shadows you were just talking about."

"Show no weakness. Show him that you won't be pushed around, that's what your father did. If he sees he can push you and get you to do what he wants, he will. It'll be cathartic in a way."

"Wait. Wait. Wait. What the hell does cathartic mean?"

"I'll be right outside."

Masato bowed then opened the office doors to be greeted by Oswald. Masato gave a small bow then stepped aside to allow Oswald in then left closing the doors behind him. Oswald walked in and looked around the office.

"You haven't done much different with the place."

"Haven't had the chance yet. I'm thinking a big ass shark tank over there," Devon said, standing and walking around the desk to shake Oswald's hand. "What can I do for you?"

"Just a casual meet and greet. Figured it was time I met the new runner of Hyde pharmaceuticals. Your father and I worked closely on several endeavors. I hope to work with you in the near future."

"It would be an honor."

"So what's on the agenda for the new boss?" Oswald asked, with a smile.

"Well, development has a leg up on a new drug for high blood pressure. Nothing too exciting."

"No game changers yet," Oswald laughed. "I'm anxious to see what a fresh young mind can do with such a company. As I said, I just want to stop by and get acquainted. If there is anything you need don't hesitate to call me."

"Thank you."

Oswald shook Devon's hand again then headed for the door. He pulled the door open then turned back to Devon.

"When you find your big breakthrough, I'd love to help you with it."

Oswald left and Masato came in and shut the doors as Devon sank down into his chair and sighed. Masato walked over and sat down in one of the chairs in front of the desk.

"He knows about the secret project. I don't think he knows that I know about it but he definitely knows," Devon said, trying to calm his nerves.

"So what's our game plan?"

Devon looked up at Masato and for the first time noticed he had changed out of his suit coat and dress shirt, he was now only wearing the sleeveless vest.

"You look a lot more comfortable now. I want a list of everyone who has access to that lab and the research notes. We need to know how many people know about this project."

"Right away, sir."

"And Masato? Are you still in contact with your demon friend? Let's give him a call, we may need help."

"A vision sir?"

"A bad one," Devon said, after a moment.

Logan

Emma pulled her SUV up to the point on her GPS and put it into park. She looked out the windshield at the naked form lying out on the end of the dock. The marina was deserted, which was to be expected seeing as it was nearly one in the morning. She reached into the back seat and grabbed a blanket she kept for emergencies and climbed out of the car. She walked down the short path and hopped the fence to the marina.

She approached the body already sure it was Logan. She knew he wasn't dead, she could see him breathing. She nudged him with her foot but got no response.

"Logan," she said, covering his lower body with the blanket. "Logan, wake up."

She shook him and he began to stir. Finally pulling himself out of his coma, he looked up at her with a confused expression. She felt a pang in her heart, he looked so pitiful lying here stark naked and confused.

"Where the hell am I?"

"The marina. Come on, we need to get you out of here," Emma said, as a faint siren could be heard.

"How did you find me?" Logan asked, as Emma helped him to his feet.

"My tiny, secret spy device I put in your arm last month. It notified me when you didn't move for five minutes."

"God, this thing must go off all the time."

"For a sloth demon, you're not very slothful. Most of the time. There are days when you hardly move," she said, unlatching the gate so he wouldn't have to climb over.

"Those are the days I'm proud of."

He climbed into the passenger seat and buckled. Emma climbed in and started the car and began backing up.

"Hey. Let's hit the little wing joint on the way home. I'm hungry."

"You and chicken wings, I swear you're going to turn into one," she said, pulling out onto the road. "How many?"

"Better make it forty. Unless you want some too."

"You're going to eat forty wings?"

"Don't judge me. It was Sheppard back there. He was buying something. I tried to get it but I couldn't take Butch."

Emma noticed Logan scratching his belly and a thin red line where he was scratching.

"What is that?"

"Butch is a person. The devil incarnate, I think..."

"Not Butch. On your stomach, where you're scratching."

"I don't know but it itches like a motherfucker."

Emma reached over and touched the place on Logan's stomach. She didn't feel anything hard beneath the skin yet it still concerned her. What had Sheppard done to him while he was out of it?

"We're going back to the house now so Hyde can look at you."

"I need my wings. I'm starving," he said, giving her the best puppy dog eyes, he could.

"You are going back to Hyde while I go get your stupid wings."

"I'll love you forever."

"Yea."

She said, feeling her heart flutter. She had never told Logan her true feelings for him and hearing him say love you made her heart skip a beat. She didn't want to risk their friendship by admitting her feelings and him not feeling the same way, where in turn things would be weird between them. She would stay his friend, his nurse when he came home with wounds, his wing run girl.

Danny

Danny came to with a start. He looked around, on his right was Tyler and in front of him were Johnny and Bruce. He instantly recognized the inside of his own car and sat back against the seat. His memory of what had happened was fuzzy. He remembered sword fighting with Johnny then everything became blurry.

"You okay?" Tyler asked.

"Yea. How long have I been out?"

"Three hours. Johnny got a call earlier and said, he had to go help a friend and that it had to do with Sheppard."

Danny sat forward and leaned over the console between the two front seats.

"Where are we and where are we going?"

"We're about an hour outside of Los Angeles."

"Why the hell are we going to LA? You know they call it the city of angels for a reason, and a car full of demons showing up is not going to be a good combination."

"Simmer down. We'll slip in and out without any issues. I promise."

"Famous last words. How are four demons going to go unnoticed in a city run by angels? Please, I want to know."

"I'm working on it."

"You're working on it. Next, you'll be saying you are going to have Bruce go into a rage fit to cause a distraction while you sneak in."

Johnny stared over at Bruce who shook his head. Danny sat back appalled that Johnny was really going to risk Bruce's life.

"You know what they'll do to me right? There is no way in hell I'm having any part of that plan," Bruce said, crossing his arms.

Lee

Lee knew he was up shit creek without a paddle, but that's how he liked life. Stealing from the Sheppards was never a good idea, but when they had something that you knew could bring you a shiny new penny you took it. Lee ran and jumped over a garbage can, landing light on his feet and kept running not bothering to look behind; he knew they were still chasing him.

Lee took a sharp right and jumped grabbing hold of the raised fire escape ladder on an apartment building and began climbing up. He glanced down at his pursuers as they struggled to grab hold of the ladder. Lee had about made it to the top when hands grabbed him and pulled him up onto the roof. He was slung down onto the ground and felt a heavy foot planted on his back.

"You fucked with the wrong people, little devil," the man holding him down said, as he reached into Lee's bag and pulled out an object wrapped in a black bag and began walking away. "Kill him."

Lee jumped to his feet and ran for the other side of the roof and leapt off the side as several gunshots tore through the night's silence and he felt two sharp pains in his back. He grabbed hold of the fire escape on the next building and made his way down as quickly as he could. Once on the ground, he took a second to catch his breath then sprinted towards his hideout where he knew he was in for a lecture, and the painful process of having the two bullets removed from his back.

Lee unlocked the door and hurried inside before anyone saw him. He stopped in the entrance hall and leaned on the wall for support.

"So!" He called.

"Where have you been? I have called you like ten times, I..." She stopped as she rounded the corner and saw the blood soaking his shirt.

"You can yell at me later. I need help right now."

"I might save you just to kill you later," she said, walking over and putting his arm around her shoulder as she walked him into the kitchen and set him down in a chair. "You know you don't have all your demon powers any more, you can't do this kind of stuff."

"I know," he said, pulling his shirt off exposing the two holes in his back.

So gathered the supplies she needed then gently cleaned the wounds and handed Lee a bottle of whiskey.

"I'm taking it, this is gonna hurt?" Lee said, opening the whiskey bottle.

"We're low on supplies. I don't have the proper equipment to do this so, yeah, it's gonna hurt like a motherfucker."

"Shit. How many more bottles of this do we have?"

"That's it."

"Goddamit," Lee said, looking at the half-full bottle in his hands then turned it up and chugged it down and burped. "Let's do it."

So stuck her makeshift tool into the first wound in Lee's

shoulder. After several minutes So was able to pull the first bullet out. She dropped the bullet into a dish on the table and wiped her brow and sighed.

"One down. You want a little breather before I dig the next one out?"

"No. Get it over with."

So stuck the tool into the pot of boiling water she had to clean it before going back in. After several minutes So had the second bullet out and had begun sewing the wounds shut. Once Lee was stitched up, she gently cleaned over the wounds and bandaged them up. While Lee didn't have all his demonic powers, he still healed a lot faster than a normal person but not as fast as he would have, had he not double-crossed a witch and been cursed.

"You can yell at me now."

"Would it do any good?" she asked, taking his hands in hers. "I can't lose you, Lee; you're all I've got."

"It'll take a lot more than this to kill me."

"Have you tried reaching out to Emma again?"

"What so she can put another curse on me? No thanks."

"Lee, it's been three years. Maybe you two could work something out, and she can remove the curse."

"Do you not remember what happened?" Lee said, standing up. "If I see that witch again, I'll kill that bitch."

"Lee. I know you are a pride demon, but you got to let that stuff go and move on. You both did each other wrong." She explained as Lee opened a bag of chocolate doughnuts on the counter.

"Are you trying to break up with me? Is that why you want me to get goodie goodie, with Emma again?"

"Never," she said, then kissed him. "Don't spoil your dinner with those."

"Okay, mom."

Danny

Danny sat impatiently in the passenger seat of Johnny's car; he looked down at his watch and sighed. He wasn't behind Johnny's plan to use Bruce as a distraction while they snuck into the city of angels. He wasn't entirely sure Johnny knew what they would do to Bruce if he was caught. Danny opened his door and got out.

"Where the hell are you going?" Johnny asked.

"I'm going to get Bruce. I'm sorry, I can't let him do this."

"I got to go with him. No offense, but I trust him more than you. I just met you," Tyler said, climbing out after Danny.

"Shit," Johnny said, hitting the steering wheel before opening his door and getting out.

Danny walked down the alley Bruce had gone down and followed it as it hit a forced left and found Bruce sitting in a chair, his hands tied behind his back. He looked unharmed, but before they could react, they felt guns pressed to the backs of their heads.

"On the ground now."

"Okay. Take it easy pal," Danny said, getting down on his knees, Tyler and Johnny following his example.

"Lie down, hands behind your backs. No funny business, there are two snipers watching your every move."

Danny and the others lay down and placed their hands behind their backs, their wrists were bound then they were frisked for weapons. Once their captor was satisfied they had no weapons, they were pulled up back onto their knees.

"It's just two guys; you guys could have taken them," Bruce said.

"Shut up," their captor said, to Bruce then he addressed the others. "Stand up. We're gonna take you to Aramis to decide what to do with four demons in our city."

"Listen, we don't want any trouble. We're just here..."

"Save it for Aramis," the guy said, pulling Danny to his feet and shoving him forward towards the abandon looking warehouse before them.

They were led inside and down into the bowels of the building, the only part of the building that seemed to have power. They were led into a large room that just looked like a very spacious living room; there were a TV, couch, and several chairs. Set up in the far-left corner was a makeshift kitchen and refrigerator.

"Knees," the second captor said, pushing Tyler down, then Johnny.

"Aramis. We have some uninvited guests. Demons."

"Thank you, Simon," Aramis said, turning around to face their captives.

Aramis wasn't at all what Danny had been expecting, he didn't look so tough, and neither did Simon. Danny found himself regretting not just beating the shit out of these guys and taking Bruce.

"I can see it on your face. Not what you were expecting

as far as angels go? We were equally disappointed. You demons aren't too fearsome."

"Untie me and I'll fuck your scrawny ass up," Johnny said.

"This one has some fire in him," Simon said, leaning against one of the chairs. "And a big mouth."

"Aramis, right? Listen we didn't come here to cause any trouble. We came to help a friend of his," Danny nodded down to Johnny. "That's it."

"A friend? Tell me, how does a demon have a friend in the city of angels?"

Johnny didn't answer; instead, he just glared at their captor that would have caused him to burst into flame if looks could kill.

"Answer me."

Johnny spit in Aramis' face then said, some obscenities in Chinese. Aramis wiped his face off then grabbed Johnny by the shirt and lifted him up, with a strength you wouldn't have thought the guy would have.

"Answer me or I'll bitch slap you back to Bangkok or wherever the hell your little Asian ass is from."

"Mileski," Johnny finally said.

"The seer?"

"Yes. Kato contacted me, saying Devon was in trouble."

"Why didn't you say so sooner?" Aramis said, letting go of Johnny then motioned Simon over. "Cut them loose."

"That's it?" Danny asked, as his hands were unbound.

"What, did you think I was going to turn you over to the angelic council?" Aramis laughed. "We're exiled angels, no more welcome in the city than you four."

"Well, this worked out," Bruce said, after being untied

from the chair he was bound to. "Ain't none of us motherfuckers welcome in this city."

"I never said, that. We're always up for some fun." Aramis said, walking over to a bookshelf and moving one of the books.

The wall beside the bookshelf rose up revealing a secret room that was filled with all sorts of weapons, guns, bows, and others Danny didn't recognize. Aramis leaned against the bookshelf with a smile.

"We'll help you if you let us join your cause to stop the Sheppard guy."

Danny looked confused for a moment then remembered they had captured Bruce earlier. Danny looked over at Bruce who smiled and shrugged.

"I have a big mouth," Bruce said.

"You could use our help, just ask the Asian over there about my strength." Aramis said, with a laugh. "We can help each other."

Logan

Hyde set several tools on his bedside worktable, he was getting ready to open Logan's stomach up and remove whatever it was that was showing up on the x-rays. He pulled on a pair of gloves and began numbing the area.

"What do you need me to do?" Emma asked.

"Rub this over his stomach, all over. With his rapid healing, we want to make sure the area I'm going to cut is as sterile as possible."

Emma applied the scrub liberally and rubbed it on. After a few minutes, she used a clean towel to dry Logan's belly. Hyde motioned for her to do it a second time, so she did, following the same procedure. Once she had Logan's belly dried off again, Hyde set about beginning his work. He made an incision then used another tool to enter Logan's stomach.

Going by the x-ray images, Hyde carefully dug in until he reached the foreign object. He gently grabbed hold of it then slowly began to pull the tool from Logan's belly, then deposited the silver object into a metal pan on the table. He grabbed a clean towel and wiped over the incision then watched as the cut healed.

"What the hell is that?" Emma asked, looking at the object.

"My guess, some sort of tracking device," Hyde said, picking up the thing and turning it over in his hand.

"Why would Sheppard want to track Logan?"

"I think a better question would be: does he now know where we are hidden?" Hyde said, dropping the tracker into a baggie and sticking it into his pocket. "I'll take it away; you need to be here when he wakes up. You told him about how you feel yet?"

"No. And that's not really any of your business."

"I'm just saying, he's a catch and if you don't hurry up and make a move someone else might."

"Are you implying that you are going to ask him out?" Emma asked, with a smile.

"Please, I don't roll that way. You two were made for each other, I just don't want you to wait too long and someone else gets him. The sob story you told me about how you two met, and everything you have been through since, you need to make your move."

"Thanks, Mom."

"All right, I'm gonna go rid ourselves of this thing. He'll be out for at least another ten minutes, so play with him if you want to."

"You are sick."

"You think if the tables were turned, he wouldn't want to take a peek at the sacred temple?"

"Get out of here."

Hyde left laughing. She heard him get in his car and drive away. She couldn't help but think about what Hyde had said; did she really need to worry about Logan hooking up with some other girl? Did he feel about her the way she did about him? If it had been her lying there would he have stayed at her side until she woke up, or as Hyde put it, took a peek at her sacred temple? Emma sighed and glanced around the room to make sure no one was around then lifted the waistband of Logan's underwear and looked beneath them.

Taka

Taka paced the room. He wasn't at all happy about the situations he found himself in. His ranks had been reduced from fifty-seven to three in one day. He had been forced to watch as his whole clan was slaughtered before his eyes while he sat helplessly.

"We should kill them all, here and now," Michael said, leaning against the wall with his arms crossed.

"Just the three of us wouldn't stand a chance, plus Judah is drunk off his ass."

"So what we just let them get away with slaughtering all our brothers?"

"No. We play along with Dana's little game until we have a solid plan. The question we need to be asking ourselves is who isn't in Sheppard's pocket?"

"The demons."

"It'll be a cold day in hell before I work alongside demons," Taka said. "Or angels"

"The lycans are fence riders."

"Who hates witches more than we do?"

"The vampires," Michael said, with a smile as he caught onto Taka's plan.

"Set me up a meeting with the elders, discretely," Taka said, sitting down on the foot of the bed Judah was passed out on. "It's time we start a war."

Lee

Lee lay on the bed on his side as Soo changed the bandages on his back. While she was busy cleaning his wounds, Lee hooked up the hard drive he had stolen from the Sheppard lab to his laptop.

"So how did you manage that one?" Soo asked.

"Make them watch this hand and not this one," Lee said. "They took the blank hard drive from my backpack while this one was in my pocket."

"You, sneaky snake," Soo laughed taping the last bandage in place and kissing his bare shoulder.

"Now to see what Sheppard has been up to."

As Lee glanced through the files, he saw several with the same titles just different numbers attached to the ends. The two files he saw most repetitive were titled, 'Necrophagous' and 'Phoenix'. He scrolled back up to the top and hovered over the first Necrophagous file.

"What do you think Necrophagous means?" Lee asked, as Soo laid her head on his shoulder.

"Only one way to find out."

Lee opened the file and was thrown into a text file that stretched on for over forty-five pages. He skimmed through the first couple pages then backed out and moved on to the next. Each file he opened seemed to consist of more research notes and scientific mumbo jumbo that made little to no sense to him. Finally, he opened a video file.

"Maybe this will tell us something."

The video opened with a man lying on a gurney surrounded by several doctors. There was an IV looking machine rigged up with several silver canisters attached to it off to the right of the gurney and the tubes were linked to an IV in the man's arm. 'Subject five has shown no signs of aggression or mutation. The Necro has been introduced twice and today will mark his fifth dose. Other subjects showed signs of aggression and or mutation after the initial dose.'

The man talking moved into the frame and gently opened the man's eyes, to show the man's eyes which were gray and cloudy. 'Let's begin the infusion.' the man said, and one of the other doctors turned on the IV looking machine. Instantly veins could be seen standing out against the man's pale skin. The veins unfurled like sleeping snakes across the man's flesh, black and appearing everywhere.

"What the hell is this?" Soo asked, watching the disturbing video.

"Sheppards doing what Sheppards do, playing God."

The man on the video began to thrash around violently as the black veins continued to spread all over his body. The restraints holding him down looked as though they would snap at any moment. The man opened his mouth and emitted a yell that sent chills down both Lee and Soo's spines. His face and neck began to split open, starting just below his nose and opening up all the way down to collar bone, a new horizontal mouth that was lined with several rows of serrated teeth.

The man began jerking violently again and blood began spilling onto the floor from underneath him. A spider-like appendage began to slither out from under him, then another, and another. 'Clear the room!' the doctor yelled as a fourth appendage emerged from the man's back. The man on the gurney finally broke free and stood up on wobbly legs. Sudden gunfire caused Lee and Soo to jump, as bullets tore the abomination apart.

"I apologize for all the times I questioned you about your desire to shut these people down. However, I'm also scared for you to continue. What if they catch you and do stuff like that to you?"

Lee rolled over onto his back with a wince and pulled her closer. Soo laid her head on his chest as he hugged her close.

"I have to stop them so they can't do that to other people."

"That's the one quality that you have that I love and hate. You have such a big heart; you put everyone else before yourself."

"But no one before you," Lee said, kissing the top of Soo's head.

Masato

Masato waited outside the office building, waiting for Johnny to show. He checked his watch; Johnny was already five minutes late. Masato was just about to turn and head back inside when a van pulled up to the curb. The side door slid open and Johnny climbed out followed by several others.

"Took you long enough," Masato said, pulling Johnny into a one arm hug. "Who are these guys?"

"My new friends it would seem. There are Danny, Tyler, Aramis, Simon and this asshole," Johnny said, pointing out each person.

"Really? My name is Bruce."

"I know; asshole fits you better though."

"Devon is upstairs. This way."

They followed Masato into the building then into the elevator. After the long ride up to the top floor, they followed Masato into a large waiting room.

"Danny," Johnny said, motioning for Danny to follow. "The rest of you stay here."

Danny followed Johnny and Masato through a set of double doors and into Devon's office. Devon was sitting behind his desk. Danny got from the look of the guy he wasn't someone who got easily frazzled, but looked as if he were sitting on pin and needles. Darren stood as they made their way over to the desk.

"Johnny, I presume."

"I am," Johnny said, shaking Devon's hand. "This is a friend of mine, Danny."

"Pleasure," Devon said, shaking Danny's hand. "I don't know how much Mr. Kato filled you in on, but our situation is dire."

"He informed me on your visit from Oswald and vaguely mentioned a secret project your father had hidden from the Sheppard Empire. Tell me of this secret project."

Devon looked at Masato who nodded.

"You can trust my friend. Masato and I go way back, and if there is someone who hates the Sheppards more than the three of us, it's my friend Danny here."

"What's your beef with the Sheppards?" Devon asked Danny.

"I wasn't always a demon," Danny said, after a moment, "The Sheppards made me what I am. I was their lab rat until I escaped."

"What were they trying to do to you?"

"He's the closest we have ever seen to an Archdemon," Johnny answered for Danny. "So that begs the question, what are the Sheppards real motives, what are they trying to make?"

"I fear the end of all we know," Devon said, opening a drawer on his desk and pulling out a thick file. "Project Phoenix."

Johnny grabbed the file and opened it. He skimmed the first couple of pages but couldn't make much sense of any of it.

"And this is?"

"In short, a cure-all. A way to rid the world of disease. Upon further research, it has some severe negative effects."

"Negative how?" Danny asked.

"Mutations."

Danny zoned out at the mention of mutations as his memory became a jumbled mess of flashbacks. Things he didn't have a memory of from his time locked away in Sheppard's lab began to surface. He saw himself tied to a gurney as doctors injected him with large syringes filled with some mysterious liquids. He saw strange creatures, once human now deformed monsters. He saw memories from his childhood, but they felt artificial like they had been rendered to give him the illusion he was there.

"Danny!" Johnny called shaking Danny's shoulders.

Danny came to and looked around at first not knowing where he was, and then everything began to make sense again. He rubbed his forehead and stood up.

"I need some air."

Johnny followed Danny to the door and pointed to Tyler and mouthed 'Stay with him'. Tyler got up and followed Danny out and onto the elevator.

"Wait. You're going to leave me alone with these two again? They said, they were gonna anal probe me earlier when they captured me," Bruce said, to Johnny.

"I thought you were gay, anyway?"

"I'm bisexual."

"What's the difference?" Johnny said, then closed the door.

Simon slid over and put his arm around Bruce's shoulders while Aramis leaned against the reception desk flirting with the receptionist.

"I'm inclined to believe this has something to do with what they did to him," Johnny said, closing the file.

"Take it. I'll feel much better knowing it's not here next time Oswald decides to make an appearance."

"Play him. Stay on his good side. We'll be in touch," Johnny said, putting the file in his bag.

"One more thing. The secret lab where my father was working on making it a cure-all and not a weapon is about thirty- two stories below your feet."

"Good to know. Any other visits or correspondence from Oswald don't hesitate to let us know. We're here to help, although with Masato around I'd say you are in good hands."

"Thank you," Devon said.

Danny stepped outside and leaned over with his hands on his knees and took several deep breaths until he felt a hand on his back. He looked over to see Tyler beside him.

"You okay?"

"I just needed to get some air. I'm fine."

"Danny, there's something I've needed to tell you for a while now," Tyler said, then took a second to think of the best way to say what he needed to. "I need to tell you..."

"You guys better get this little psycho. I'm gonna go all kinds of levels of Kung Fu on his ass," Bruce said, barreling through the doors of the office building.

"I just want a hug," Simon said, with a laugh.

"We gotta go. We've been in the city too long as it is. We're lucky no angels have caught onto us," Johnny said, heading for the van.

"What were you saying?" Danny asked, standing up.

"It can wait," Tyler said, with a smile. "Let's get out of here."

Lee

Lee rolled over in bed; he knew he had heard something. He gently woke Soo then walked over to a large painting on the wall and pulled it away to reveal a safe. He quickly put in the combination then pulled it open and pulled out a pistol. He slowly opened the bedroom door and stepped out into the hall. He slowly made his way down the hall as he heard movement and quiet talking coming from the living room. He made it to the end of the hall then took a deep breath then rounded the corner aiming the gun at the intruders.

"What the fuck are you doing here?" Lee said, aiming at the Girl standing beside the sofa where a guy was lying.

"Woah, Woah! Take it easy Lee."

"Get the hell out, now."

"Lee," Soo said, putting her hand on his to lower the gun. "It's okay."

Soo walked over and gave the girl a hug then looked down at the guy on the couch.

"What happened?"

"We drugged him. Sheppard had placed a tracker in him. We removed it and Hyde has taken it to dispose of it. We couldn't risk staying if Sheppard knew where we were."

"It's okay," Soo said, then turned back to Lee. "Lee, let's

be civil here."

"Nice yellow undies," Emma said, looking at Lee.

Lee looked down at his yellow boxer briefs, in his rush to keep Soo safe he hadn't even bothered to put on any clothes and now here he was standing in nothing but his underwear with a pistol in his hand.

"I'm gonna go put something on," Lee said, turning to leave.

Emma watched him as he walked away until Soo socked her in the arm.

"You have a boyfriend lying here on my couch, stop staring at mine."

"Sorry," she said, with a laugh. "Can we stay here for a few days?"

"Of course. Seems as if everyone is having their run in's with Oswald these last few days."

"You guys?"

"I pulled three bullets from Lee's back earlier after he stole a hard drive from a Sheppard lab. I am very surprised he didn't lose his shit seeing you here."

"That did go a lot smoother than I thought it would. What have you done to the Lee I dated?"

"Tread lightly. I brought you up earlier and he did flip his lid. Let's just all try to get along."

"No problem."

Lee came back out of the bedroom and went to the kitchen where he poured himself a glass of water. He started back to the bedroom but Soo stopped him.

"Lee, let's all agree to get along for now while we are staying together. Okay?"

"Fine," Lee said, though Soo could tell he wasn't happy.

Emma stuck her hand out to Lee waiting on him to shake it.

"So you can curse me again?" Lee said, not taking her hand.

"Geeze, I'm trying to take the first step here so we can put all this behind us. What is it going to take to get you to forgive me?"

"Remove the curse."

"You know I can't. I use that kind of magic and the coven will know exactly where I am."

"Talk to me when you're not too much of a pussy to reverse the wrong you've done," Lee said, walking back to the bedroom.

"Sorry," Soo said, as Lee closed the bedroom door.

"No. He's right. We both did some shitty ass stuff to each other but I did go too far when I cursed him."

"You guys get some rest. Make yourselves at home. There's food in the kitchen, blankets, and pillows in the locker over there."

"Thank you, Soo."

Oswald

Oswald looked over the papers in his hands as he rode the elevator down to the lab. He had spent years and billions of dollars trying to recreate the Phoenix project. He resented Mileski for pulling the plug on the project then sealing away the files so as to never be found. It had cost the Sheppard empire a fortune.

"Good evening sir." One of the scientists said, as the elevator doors opened.

"Is everything ready to move forward?" Oswald asked, handing the scientist the papers as he walked into the observation room.

"Subject 856 is prepped and ready. Waiting on your word."

Oswald looked out through the three-foot thick glass at the man strapped to the gurney.

"Let's do it."

Oswald watched as the virus was introduced to the man, the violent jerking and writhing began almost immediately. The man had fully mutated in under three minutes, a new record. Oswald sighed, it was easy enough to make monsters, harder yet to make someone immune to the virus.

"Impressive." A voice came from behind Oswald.

"Uncle Alexander. I didn't know you were going to be coming by."

"This is the Phoenix project?"

"Our version of it."

"I admire your progress. What is your timeline for global release?"

"Hard to tell. We still don't know what the effects could be on other species besides humans."

"You have most of them under your thumb. Start the testing. We need results, nephew, or they will be swift to replace you."

"Yes, sir."

Logan

Logan woke up lying on the couch; he looked around trying to figure out where he was. Emma noticed he was awake and walked over and sat down on the couch.

"How you feel?"

"Okay. Where are we?"

"A friend's. That thing in your belly was a tracker. Sheppard could have already raided our hideout by now. There's no pain where we removed it is there?"

Emma pushed his shirt up and gently pressed around on his belly to make sure he didn't have any pain.

"I gotta pee," Logan said, jumping up and walking fast towards where he assumed the bathroom was.

He shoved past Lee as he came out of the bathroom nearly shoving Lee over.

"What's your problem?"

"I have an erection."

"Okay, weirdo. You better clean up after yourself in there."

Lee went into the kitchen and kissed Soo who was making breakfast. He poured himself a glass of milk and sat down at the table.

"He okay?" Emma asked, sitting down.

"You gave him a boner. He's in the bathroom taking care of it," Lee said, not looking at Emma.

Emma smiled trying her hardest not to laugh. She glanced back over her shoulder to the bathroom to see if he was coming yet or not.

"Why don't you go help him with it?" Lee said, sarcastically

"Maybe I will," Emma said, standing up and walking back to the bathroom and walked right in, Logan hadn't locked the door.

"What are you doing. I..."

Logan was cut off as Emma closed the door. Lee stared ahead towards the bathroom shocked. He hadn't thought she would actually do it. He turned around to look at Soo,

"We're going to need to clean that bathroom a hundred times over when they are done." Lee said.

Several minutes later they emerged from the bathroom, Logan with a cheesy grin on his face. They sat down at the table and everyone remained in awkward silence.

"Did you swallow?" Lee asked.

"Oh, my God, Lee!" Soo said, shocked.

"This is getting weird. Next, y'all are going to be talking about the size of my penis. Can we just eat breakfast?"

"Yes," Soo said, before Lee or Emma could go at each other again. "We have eggs, toast..."

The door to Lee and Soo's hideout burst open with an explosion. Lee grabbed his pistol he kept hidden under the table as the smoke cleared. Butch and several of Sheppard's hired guns entered.

"Well, lookie here. Four for the price of two," Butch said. "Our little tracker led us to your other hideout and the little doctor we found there led us here."

"Hyde," Emma whispered.

"Sheppard did want you alive. Until he realized how much of a pain in the ass you are. Now we're here to exterminate you."

The hired guns raised their guns and began firing. Lee dove to shield Soo as bullets tore their little home apart. Lee felt several bullets hit him in the back as he and Soo collapsed to the floor and a faint orange glow illuminated around the four of them. Emma had created a shield around them. Lee looked down at Soo who lay motionless beneath him; he felt warm blood against his chest and noticed the bullet hole in Soo's neck.

Lee felt his heart drop as his brain tried to comprehend that Soo was dead. Warm tears began spilling from his eyes as he gently shook her and called her name. Once the realization finally set in, so did rage. Lee stood up and tried to leave the shield around them to rip all Sheppard's men to shreds.

"Lee, you can't leave."

"Let me out of this goddamn thing!" Lee said, punching the barrier in front of him.

"Lee, calm down," Emma said, noticing the men planting explosives around the room.

"Let me out!" Lee said, aiming his pistol at the barrier.

"Lee, if you break the barrier, we'll all die," she said, feeling a lump form at the back of her throat; she had never seen Lee so broken, and even if all they did was fight a part of her still loved him. "Logan, hold him."

Logan grabbed Lee and forced him down onto the ground. Even in his rage, he was no match for Logan's strength. Had he not have been cursed and had all his powers it would have been a different story.

"Let's see you survive a building coming down on your heads," Butch said, touching Emma's barrier. "You're a half witch, your barrier won't hold much longer, or that much weight coming down on you."

Butch and his men filed out as Emma used all her strength to keep the barrier as solid as possible. She hoped she was strong enough for them to survive this. A few moments later, the bombs went off and the building collapsed down on top of them. Emma struggled to hang on, she could feel her strength giving way and when it did, they would surely be crushed.

The barrier began to shrink, closing in around them. She knew Butch had been right. She was only a half witch and her powers were nothing compared to a real witch. Just when Emma thought they were done for, the rubble covering them was cleared away by some invisible force. Emma's barrier faded as the last of the debris was moved away. Standing above them at street level was Taka, Judah, and Michael.

Logan let go of Lee who had given up fighting a while ago and got to his feet, surprised as Emma to see their rescuers.

"Looks like you guys could use a hand," Taka said, jumping down to help them out.

"You have no idea," Emma said, as Taka lifted her up to Judah and Michael.

Logan gently grabbed Lee under the arms and pulled him over.

"What's wrong with him?" Taka asked.

"He's in shock, I think. That was his girlfriend."

"Shit," Taka said, looking over at Soo's body. "Let's get him up then we'll get her out of here. Judah! Rope from the car."

Judah ran to their car and retrieved the rope from the trunk and tossed one end down to Taka. Taka tied the rope around Lee then gave Michael the thumbs up and Lee was pulled up. Taka then walked over to Soo's body and gently carried her over. Once Lee was up and untied, Judah, tossed the rope back over and Soo was tied up and pulled up.

"You next," Taka said, to Logan as he held his hands out, his fingers interlaced.

Logan stepped up onto Taka's hand and Taka lifted Logan up to where Michael could grab his hands and pull him up. Once Logan was up, Taka walked back a few paces then ran and jumped, just high enough for Michael to grab his wrists and Michael pulled him up.

"Thank you," Emma said, as Taka sat down.

"What's the last you've heard about the witches' coven?"

"Nothing since I left three years ago."

"War is coming. The coven plans to start a war with Sheppard, Sheppard plans to start a war with the world and we're going to try and wipe them both out before they can start their wars," Taka explained. "Dana slaughtered all my warlocks, right before us as we were helpless under her spells."

"I'm sorry, Taka."

"We're recruiting, so we can start a war to end theirs before it starts. I have a meeting with the Vampire elders tonight. I know you know plenty of people who hate the Sheppards, we could use all the help we can get."

"We should move before someone sees us," Michael said, picking up Soo's body.

"He's right. Butch and his goons could still be around," Emma explained. "I'll join your fight and I'll see who else I can get."

Judah picked up Lee and put him over his shoulder and they set off for the last safe house Emma had, a cabin hidden deep in the woods.

Danny

Danny had just dozed off in the back seat as the van came to an abrupt stop; he was jerked forward and snapped awake.

"Shit," Aramis said, leaning forward to look out the windshield.

"All right, this is where you guys come in," Johnny said, looking at Aramis in the rearview mirror.

"Us? If we get caught, we are as dead as you guys," Aramis said, looking out the back window.

They were blocked in both directions. Somehow, the angels had learned of their presence in the city and had shown up to make them pay for crossing over into their territory. Danny counted seven, they were only outnumbered by one, but the thing was Danny had never fought an angel before and had no idea what they would be going up against.

"Can we fight our way out?" Bruce asked.

"I don't think we have any other option," Simon said, unzipping one of the weapons bags.

They all grabbed a weapon from the bag and stepped out of the van. Danny could tell Tyler was nervous standing beside him. As long as he had known Tyler, which had been most of his life, Danny knew Tyler wasn't a big fighter.

"Hey," Danny said, getting Tyler's attention. "When I

tell you to, I want you to smack the flat of your sword into Bruce's face."

"What?"

"Trust me. Let's make a rage demon mad."

"You sure about this?"

"It's better than the alternative, which is them killing us. Hit him."

Tyler took a deep breath and took the sword in both hands and pulled it back then swung with all his strength bringing the flat of the sword into Bruce's face. Bruce stumbled back grabbing his broken nose and dropping his weapon. He looked at his hand which was covered in blood then looked up at Tyler with a look of confusion.

"I don't think it worked," Tyler said.

Johnny caught onto their plan and punched Bruce in the face. Bruce went down to the ground and Johnny began kicking him.

"Come on little gay boy, fight back," Johnny said, continuing to kick Bruce. "Nobody likes you. You're a little pussy bitch!"

"What the fuck are you guys doing?" Aramis asked.

"Enough!" One of the angels said, stepping forward.

The angel walked over pacing back and forth in front of them. He was wearing armor of gold and white, his arms like tree trunks coming off his chiseled body. He stopped in front of Danny.

"I take it you're the leader," he said, and then with amazing speed for his size he drew his sword and thrust it into Danny's stomach.

Danny gasped as the warm metal pierced his stomach and threatened to burst through his back. Danny looked up at the angel, blood beginning to fill his mouth and spill over his lip.

"Does it hurt? Holy steel. It's warm, isn't it? Now I know this wound won't kill you, we have a proposition for you. Your friends can leave, if they all use their weapons to strike you down."

Tyler dropped the sword he had been holding and got down on his knees.

"You'll have to kill me too."

"And me," Bruce said, walking over and dropping to his knees beside Tyler.

After a moment, Johnny joined them, then Aramis and Simon. The angel holding the sword in Danny's gut smiled then pulled the blade out. Danny dropped to his knees holding the gushing wound.

"It's admirable the way you demons stick together, even corrupted two angels in the process," the angel said, then turned to his men. "Kill them."

"You harm... one hair... on any of their heads..."

"You'll what? You have a hole in your gut, you're bleeding profusely."

Danny tried his hardest to summon the darkness within him, to will the snake-like demons from within him to come out. They very slowly began to materialize.

"Danny, stop! You don't have the strength right now," Johnny pleaded.

Danny continued anyway. He could feel himself getting weaker as he tried to will the demons forward. Danny felt a fresh gush of blood from the wound in his stomach that didn't seem to be healing.

"Enough of this," the angel said, and swung the sword

and connecting it with Danny's neck.

"NO!" Tyler yelled as the blade went nearly halfway through Danny's neck.

The angel pulled the sword free and Danny collapsed to the ground in a pool of blood. Bruce felt himself losing control and he made no effort to contain it. His eyes turned a bright red. He grabbed the sword Tyler had dropped and jumped to his feet, and bolted for the angel that had killed Danny. He drove the sword between the man's shoulders then climbed up onto the angel's back and grabbed his head and used all his strength and tore his head clean off. Johnny grabbed his katana he had dropped and set about taking on several other angels.

"Get Danny into the van. You know where to take him," Aramis said, to Simon as he grabbed a weapon and joined the fray.

Simon helped Tyler get Danny loaded into the van then they sped away, crashing through the angel's barricade. Johnny had never personally seen a rage demon in action, and now that he was it was fairly terrifying. Bruce seemed to have gained massive strength and a thirst for blood; he was literally ripping these men limb from limb.

Once they were in the clear, Bruce sat down breathing heavily as his eyes turned back to their normal color. Johnny sheathed his katana and put a hand on Bruce's shoulder.

"You are one badass motherfucker when you go into beast mode."

"Danny?"

"I got him on his way to someone who may be able to help him. Come on, we got a good walk ahead of us."

Johnny offered Bruce a hand and pulled him to his feet.

"You know I didn't mean any of that shit earlier right. Was just trying to get you mad."

Tyler and Simon carried Danny into the house, Tyler wasn't sure what exactly they were doing here, they were back on the outskirts of town in an abandoned house. They laid Danny on the kitchen table and then Simon took off deeper into the house.

"Kyler!" Simon yelled as he disappeared.

Simon found the basement door and descended down into the bowels of the house where he found Kyler leaned over a fresh corpse laid out on his exam table. Simon walked over and pulled one of the earbuds out of Kyler's ear.

"Good thing I'm not here to kill you."

"What are you doing here? Aramis with you?"

"No. But we need your help. I've got a guy upstairs that is on death's doorstep."

"Okay," Kyler said, dropping the tool he was using and began running around the room gathering up supplies and tossing them into a bag. "What happened?"

"He was stabbed. These guys said, they were angels but they didn't look like any angels I've ever seen. Said his sword was holy steel."

"This patient a demon?"

"Yes. Pick up the pace, he's up there dying."

Simon and Kyler emerged from the basement and entered the kitchen where Tyler was pressing his hands over the wound in Danny's stomach. Kyler ran over and set his bag down on the counter and opened it. He pulled out a pair of scissors and held them out to Tyler.

"Get that shirt off of him," Kyler said, after Tyler took

the scissors. "When you're done, go wash your hands — both of you. I'm gonna need help."

Tyler got Danny's shirt cut open then went over to the sink and scrubbed his hands down. Tyler had felt fear before, for others and for his own life at times but this somehow felt different, he was genuinely scared Danny wasn't going to make it.

"First thing I want to know, is how, demon or not, is someone with these types of wounds still alive?" Kyler asked, tossing each of them a pair of blue rubber gloves.

"According to his buddies, he's an archdemon," Simon said, pulling on his gloves.

"An archdemon? Tell me why I shouldn't do the world a favor and just let him bleed out here."

"He's my brother, and I haven't had the chance to tell him yet. We demons aren't what everyone makes us out to be, most of us anyway. If there ever was a good demon, it's Danny. He'd give you the shirt off his back, no matter what species or clan you are from. We're made out to be these evil, minions of the devil — creatures — and we're not. There's a difference between demons," Tyler said, patting his chest. "And your religious demons. Two very different things. I'm not here to try and change your opinion on us, but please save my brother."

Kyler nodded and leaned in to look at the wound in Danny's gut. The edges of the wound were gray, slowly turning black. Kyler gently touched the edge of the hole and the skin around the hole was ice cold.

"Holy steel?" Kyler asked, looking up at Simon.

"That's what he said."

"This wasn't holy steel. The blade he was stabbed with

80

was hexed. I have to make a call," Kyler said, taking his gloves off.

"Wh..." Tyler began.

"You brother is cursed. You see this," Kyler said, pointing to the blackening skin around the wound. "'It's spreading. I can't lift curses, but I know someone who can. Now what I need you to do is cover the wound with a sterile bandage from my bag. Simon, go downstairs and grab all the heating patches I have in the metal locker. Stick them all over his body; the heat will slow the spreading."

Tyler dug through Kyler's bag and pulled out a bandage and gently placed it over the wound as Simon returned with an armload full of heating patches. They began opening them and placing them all over Danny's upper body.

"She's on her way," Kyler said, walking back into the kitchen.

"How far away is she?" Tyler asked.

"An hour."

"And how long does he have?" Simon asked, sticking on another heat patch.

"Optimistically..." Kyler lifted the bandage and looked at the spreading curse. "Hour and a half."

Danny sat upright gasping for breath, his body covered in sweat. He turned and sat on the edge of the bed catching his breath. The dream was always the same; he was back in Sheppard's lab beneath Tucson. He got up and walked to the bathroom where he splashed some cold water onto his face. He looked at himself in the mirror; he still had a faint pink scar on the left side of his chest. A slowly fading reminder of what Oswald had done to him.

He walked back out into the room, glad to see he hadn't woken Piper with his fit. After escaping Sheppard's grasp in Tucson, Danny had fled as far as he could to try and get his chance at a normal life. Danny knew he could never reverse what Oswald had done to him; he just had to find a way to live with it, to control it. Danny sat down on the edge of the bed again trying to clear his mind. He felt a gentle touch on his back.

"You okay?" Piper asked, rubbing his back. "Another dream?"

"Yeah."

"I'll make you some tea. It'll help settle your nerves." She said, then kissed the back of his neck and climbed out of bed.

After a minute, Danny got up and headed downstairs. He rounded the corner and walked over to the island and sat down as Piper fixed the tea.

"We got the party at the museum tonight; did you decide what you are going to wear?"

"Yeah. That black shirt you like me to wear."

"You look good in it," she said, setting a cup on the island in front of him. "I'm excited to get to show you off to all my girlfriends."

"They still think I'm made up?" Danny chuckled.

"They do. I tell them how perfect you are."

"I'm perfect?"

"Perfect for me," she said, and leaned over the island and kissed him. "Oh! 'Don't forget..."

The French doors behind Danny burst with an explosion then gunfire broke through their peaceful morning.

Danny was jerked away from his memories, though his eyes were open he couldn't make out any of the people surrounding him as he gasped for breath that just didn't want to come. He felt his vision going black again.

"He's going back," a female voice said.

Danny got to his hands and knees, his ears ringing from the explosion. He shook his head and stumbled to his feet.

"Piper!" Danny called as he made his way around the island.

He could feel jagged pieces of glass in his back as he rounded the island then all his pain was forgotten. Lying on the floor was Piper, two gunshot wounds to her chest. Danny heard movement from the shattered door and turned to see a man with a rifle aimed at him.

"Down on your knees."

Danny bit back his rage and dropped to his knees. The man kept the rifle aimed at him as he walked in and over to Danny.

"Should have stayed in your cage, Carter."

Danny waited for that momentary drop in his guard them attacked. He grabbed the man's arm and flipped him onto his back then began punching him in the face repeatedly. By the time he was done, the man's skull was caved in. Danny went to stand up, but was flung forward as a shotgun blast hit him in the back.

Danny was once again jerked from his memory and into the real world. This time his vision was a little clearer. Breath came easier, but was still a painful task. He tried to sit up, but hands pushed him back down onto the table. He recognized

Tyler and Simon but none of the other people around him.

"Damn it, he's gonna slip back. Logan, give me the witch hazel."

Danny felt a cool substance being rubbed on his stomach then on his neck. He tried to sit up again but was held down once again.

"Here, put this over his nose and mouth. He keeps trying to get up and I'm gonna take two inches off his liver."

Simon placed the cloth over Danny's face. Danny shook his head trying to get the weird smelling cloth off his face. He felt someone patting his left shoulder and looked over to see Tyler.

"It's okay Danny. It's okay."

Danny's eyes started to become heavy and their voices seemed to be coming from further and further away. He heard Tyler assuring him everything was okay one last time before sleep overtook him.

Danny rolled over onto his back as the man with the shotgun entered the kitchen. Danny was on his feet and charging at the man before he knew what was happening. Danny slammed the man back against the over, knocking the gun out of his hand. He grabbed the man by the shirt and slammed him against the over several more times before letting him drop to the floor. Danny grabbed the back of the man's shirt with one hand and pulled open the dishwasher with the other. He then used the dishwasher door to smash the man's head.

Danny took a few steps back out of breath, looking at the horror movie that had become his life. He stepped over the man he had killed with the dishwasher, and sat down on the floor beside Piper. He gently pulled her into a hug as the tears began cutting tracks through the blood on his face.

Tyler

Tyler was dozing off in one of the kitchen chairs when Emma walked in and startled him awake. She gently touched his shoulder and offered him a warm smile.

"Why don't you go get cleaned up and get some rest? He's gonna be fine. He's safe here with all of us."

Tyler didn't want to but he knew she was right; he needed a shower and a few minutes of sleep. His clothes were stained in Danny's blood as were his arms and hands.

"Bathroom is down the hall on the right. I got you some of Kyler's clothes, towel, and rag in there."

"Thanks."

Tyler walked out of the kitchen and down the hall and went into the bathroom. He saw the stack of cloths on the back of the toilet along with his rag and towel. He shut the door and turned on the shower, letting it warm up. He pulled off his tee shirt and dropped it onto the floor. He grabbed the sink and looked at himself in the mirror, blood smears across his face. He turned and headed for the shower, glancing back over his shoulder at his reflection in the mirror and the vertical scar just above the waistband of his pants. After finishing getting undressed, he got into the shower, he stood under the scorching hot water and leaned his head back.

There was a lot Danny didn't know about him, and some of that he wanted to keep that way. He didn't want Danny to know what Oswald had done to him, or that he had ever been in Sheppard's lab. He debated whether or not he should tell Danny they were brothers; Danny needed to keep a level head for the long hard road ahead.

After scrubbing himself down, Tyler dried off and got dressed. He came out of the bathroom and went back to the kitchen. Danny was still asleep on the table and Bruce was sitting beside him.

"When did you guys get here?" Tyler asked.

"A few minutes ago. We couldn't come straight away; there was more of those guys following us."

"Everybody else okay?"

"Yeah," Bruce said, and pulled a pack of cigarettes from his pocket.

Bruce took one out and put it in his mouth then offered the pack to Tyler. Tyler shook his head and Bruce lit his.

"He looks rough."

"You have no idea."

"I killed them all. If it makes you feel any better," Bruce said, then took a drag from his smoke.

"A little."

"Hey! No smoking in my house."

Bruce slowly raised the cigarette back to his lips and took another puff then blew out the smoke.

"Boy, I ain't playing. Can't believe I got a house full of demons. What the hell was Simon thinking? Of all creatures, demons."

"We're right here, asswipe."

"Cursing. You need Jesus boy."

"You need Jesus," Bruce laughed.

"Smoking up in my house."

"Jesus smoked cigarettes," Bruce said.

"What kind of cigarettes did Jesus smoke?" Kyler asked, getting more worked up by the moment.

"He smoked that home rolled shit."

"These ain't cigarettes. This is ciga-weed," Kyler said, picking up the pack of cigarettes and smelling them.

"Can you go outside and smoke it?" Tyler said, trying to keep from laughing at the two of them. "We are guests here."

"Fine," Bruce said, getting up and snatching his smokes back from Kyler. "I'm gonna go smoke with Jesus."

Tyler could tell Kyler was furious. Tyler walked over and sat down in the chair Bruce had been sitting in beside Danny.

"Is it too late for me to say I don't know him?" Tyler said.

"Not devil's minions, huh?"

"That's just Bruce. He finds things that he knows he can get under your skin about and does it. Trust me, when I first met him, I didn't like him either. But underneath his 'piss everybody off' attitude, he's a good guy."

Tyler noticed Emma heading outside and wondered where she was heading. He got up and followed her out. She walked across the yard to another abandon looking house. He snuck around the side and pressed himself up against the wall by a window.

"I remember how much you love mac and cheese. Made you some," Emma said, setting the bowl on an end table beside a worn-out recliner. "Lee, come on. You have to snap out of this.

Emma dusted off a cushion on one of the chairs and sat down. She looked at Lee sitting on the floor unmoving.

"These people here, they are your best shot at getting your justice on Sheppard. They are all working together to try and bring him down. They could really use you."

"They don't need me."

"Yes, they do," Emma said, surprised he had said, anything.

Lee stood up and walked over to Emma. He grabbed the arms of the chair and leaned in.

"I'm leaving."

"Lee..." As he stood upright, she put her right hand on his chest and whispered a spell. "The least I can do."

Lee knew instantly that the spell she had put on him would grant him some protection. He took a deep breath, feeling like a thousand-pound weight had been lifted from his shoulders.

"Thank you," he said, sticking the pistol he had taken off Emma's hip in the waist of his pants.

She noticed the gun and felt her holster, empty. He turned and left. She jumped up and followed him out onto the porch.

"Lee!" She called after him as he kept walking. "Lee!"

She watched from the dilapidated porch as Lee disappeared into the woods. She sighed, cursing herself for just letting him walk away. Tyler walked around the side of the house and stood beside her.

"So what's his story?"

"I don't think there is anyone here who wants Oswald dead more than him."

"You might be surprised."

"Oswald's men slaughtered his girlfriend right in front of him. He's broken, dangerous — to anyone who gets in his way and to himself."

"Want me to go after him?"

"No. No, he would kill you without breaking a sweat. Hopefully, he will go out on his own and cope with what happened and come to his senses before he gets himself killed," she explained finally looking away from the woods. "Come on, let's go check on Danny."

"Speak of the devil," Tyler said, seeing Danny walking out of the house and into the woods.

"What is he doing up?" Emma said, as they started following him.

Danny moved silently through the woods, a predatory look on his face. He stopped abruptly. Several hundred feet ahead of him was a young buck. Danny took a few more careful steps then raised his right hand out towards the buck. A smokey gray mist formed around his back and Tyler knew what was coming. Tyler grabbed Emma's shoulder and held her back as the snake-like heads materialized out of the gray mist.

"Amazing," Emma whispered. "I didn't believe you guys when you said, he was an archdemon, but then again no one else could have survived those wounds he did."

"How much do you know about arch demons?"

"I've done my fair share of studying."

"What are those things?" Tyler whispered.

"Think of it, kind of like... split personality. Archdemons are so powerful they are split between themselves and their familiars. They are still part of him, just a different side."

"They are his dark side?"

"More or less. We all have that side of us that makes us do things and we can't really explain why our inner demons. With archdemons, that side doesn't just surface every now and then it takes on a physical form. You ever heard him having conversations with himself?"

"Once or twice."

"They talk to him, only he can hear them though."

The serpents had finally finished materializing and the right one shot forward with lightning speed and grabbed the buck by the neck and lifted it into the air then slammed it down onto the ground.

"They're weak. They are feeding to heal his body. I doubt he's even aware of what's going on right now. I've seen this before. You're not squeamish, are you?"

"No. You've seen this before?"

"I knew an archdemon, a long time ago. Once they are done feeding, he'll collapse out there. We can carry him back and clean him up before anyone else sees him."

"Clean him up?"

"What they eat, he eats. What he eats, they eat. Three mouths are better than two."

Tyler looked back out to where Danny had been, now he was on his knees leaned over the deer as the two serpents tore hunks of meat from the deer. Danny leaned back up, a chunk of bloody meat hanging out of his mouth and blood smeared across his face. Tyler looked away a bit grossed out.

"I asked if you were gonna be good with this." Emma whispered.

"I didn't know I was going to see him tearing into a deer like a wild animal."

"Touché."

Lee

Lee had waited across the street from the gun shop until five minutes before they were to close. He entered the shop and quickly glanced around; he was the only one besides the owner behind the counter. He walked over to the counter and placed his right hand on the counter with the nine-millimeter he had taken from Emma in it.

"Hit an alarm and I'll kill you right now."

The man behind the counter raised his hands and took a step back.

"What do you want?"

"Something automatic, two forty-fives and shotgun. That shotgun," Lee said, nodding to a black twelve gauge with skulls on it.

The man behind the counter got the shotgun and set it down on the counter in front of Lee. Once the man had produced the guns Lee wanted, he went to reach under the counter and Lee raised the pistol.

"What the hell did I say?"

"If you want ammo, it's under here."

Lee glanced down at the glass front of the counter where there were boxes of ammo.

"Move back. Get your goddamn ass over there," Lee

said, motioning with the pistol.

Lee walked around the counter and reached under the counter and pulled out several boxes of ammo for each gun then stuffed them into a large duffle bag along with the guns.

"Thank you for your cooperation," Lee said, as he headed for the door when the alarm began going off. "You little fucker."

Lee flipped him off before going out the door, and disappeared into the night long before the cops arrived.

Danny

As Emma had said, once the serpents had finished feeding, they dissipated and Danny collapsed to the ground. Tyler gently picked Danny up and got him into a sitting position so he and Emma could get him back to the house, but as he was sitting him up Danny woke up.

"Where am I?"

"In the woods," Tyler said,

"I thought we were in the city, and then..."

"You got stabbed, and got your throat slit and she saved you."

"Guess I owe you my thanks," Danny said, looking over at Emma.

"Can you walk?"

"Yeah," Danny said, struggling to stand up then stumbling. "I feel like I've had three forties in the last ten minutes."

"It's the medicine Kyler gave you earlier," Emma said, helping him steady himself.

They each put one of his arms around their shoulders and helped him walk back through the woods. They made it to the abandoned house where Tyler had spied on Emma and set Danny down on the porch to rest.

"I'll go get some water and rags," Emma said, heading for the other house.

"Water?"

"We got to clean you up. Your 'snake things' just went for a nice feeding," Tyler said, sitting down beside Danny. "And you did a good bit of eating too."

Danny felt his chin then looked at his hand which had blood on it.

"What the hell did I eat?"

"A deer."

"Oh God, it might be about to come back up."

Tyler slid over a little in case Danny did barf.

"You were stabbed with a cursed blade, those guys weren't angels, and Bruce totally lost his shit on them according to Johnny."

"Here you go," Emma said, walking over with a bowl of warm water and a rag.

Danny took the bowl and began wiping the blood from his face, neck, chest, and stomach. Once he was finished wiping himself off, Emma held a can of soda out to him.

"Thought you might want to get that taste out of your mouth."

Danny cracked the can open and began chugging it down. After a few seconds, Tyler tapped the bottom of the can.

"Take a breath there, bud."

Danny lowered the can and burped loudly.

"Excuse me," Danny said, tossing the empty can.

"You don't let them out very often, do you?" Emma asked, sitting down beside Danny. "What we saw out there looked like a first time feeding, but there is no way that is your first time."

"I'm not like your typical archdemon. I have this..." Danny motioned at himself, "because some asshole in a lab coat decided to test his theories on me."

"Sheppard. You fight to keep them buried within you; what if embracing them was a better course of action?"

"You've seen what they can do?"

"I have. Sometimes the only way to get to the light is to embrace the darkness," she said, then leaned back to look at Danny's back and gently touched above the waistband of his pants where the serpents seemed to come from. "How exactly do they exit your body?"

"You know as much as I do," a shiver running up his spine as she touched his back.

"I knew an archdemon a long time ago. My father. He, like you, was afraid of the power within himself. He left us when I was six, afraid that he might hurt me or my mom."

"Where is he now?"

"No clue. My point is, maybe trying to keep them caged up isn't the best thing to do. I want..."

"If I want to stick a kazoo up my ass and play a song, it doesn't concern you!" Bruce yelled storming out of the other house.

"What in the hell?" Tyler said, looking towards the house. "Bruce?"

"I'm done. Sorry to abandon you guys, but I'm going home," Bruce said, walking for the road.

Danny got to his feet and grabbed the jacket Emma had brought with her and pulled it on. He walked as fast as he could, considering his condition, to catch up with Bruce.

"Bruce," Danny called.

"Danny, go back. You don't need to be up."

"I'm okay," Danny said, looking down at the faint line where his wound had been on his stomach, then sat down on a tree that had fallen beside the road. "Are you?"

Danny could see Bruce had tears streaking down his face. Danny patted the tree beside him for Bruce to sit down. Bruce sighed and ran a hand through his hair before walking over to the tree and sitting down.

"If you don't want to talk, I understand, but I'm here to listen if you want to."

Bruce dug his pack of cigarettes from his pocket and put one between his lips and lit it, then offered Danny one. Danny took one and Bruce lit it for him. Bruce took a long drag from his cigarette then exhaled the smoke.

"You know about my sexuality?"

"You mentioned it before."

"It's caused me hell all my life. I used to get teased and jumped at school. My dad was the worst though. I was an abomination in his eyes — the gay son of a Godly family. I guess he thought he could beat it out of me," Bruce took another drag from his smoke. "Every night when he got home from work, he would start his questions, and when I didn't answer the way he wanted me to, it was seven lashings from his belt."

"Shit."

"My mom has some compassion. Though she didn't approve of my choices, I believe she still cared about me. I still see her face the day I left. My dad had gone into a particularly heavy beating and while he was winded from hitting me, I made my escape. I ran. I remember looking back over my shoulder at my parents on the porch, my dad with an almost triumphant look on his face and my mother a look of loss. Then that fucking guy in there, Kyler. He tried to hit me, calling me some of the same names my father did and I lost my shit."

"And the bit about a kazoo up your ass?"

"I say stupid shit when I'm upset," Bruce chuckled. "I'm not going to be that person again. Not who I was back then. And if that's how I'm going to be treated here then I'm leaving. I'm not going back to the depression and suicide attempts. I can't..."

Danny pulled Bruce over into a hug.

"No one is going to treat you that way again. I promise. If they do, they will answer to me. "

"Thanks, Danny."

"No sweat, buddy," Danny said, standing up. "Let's head back, get a little sleep before we have to head out."

Sheppard

Oswald entered the lab and the chatter of the workers instantly stopped. A woman in her mid-forties approached him and handed him a clipboard.

"Sir, subject 83 is showing promising results. His blood count..."

"Is he bonding or not?" Oswald asked, shoving the clipboard back to her then approaching the large window looking into the holding room.

"Not at the rate of subject 7, but yes. He's bonding."

Oswald continued staring out through the six-inch thick glass for any movement, but saw none. He looked down at his watch then back to the woman.

"When is his next scheduled feeding?"

"In an hour, sir. Ken is out getting more livestock."

"We had six cows set aside for him."

"He tore through all six in under ten minutes. We released two to begin with; he tore the feeding door off and got the other four."

"Fascinating," Oswald said, marveling over his newest success. "Be sure I am here for his next feeding. Let's really see what he's capable of."

Lee

Lee was squatted down on a rooftop several hundred feet away from the Sheppard outpost he had stumbled across. A light rain cascaded down as he looked through the scope on one of the rifles he had taken earlier. He moved the gun to get a view of the west side of the building where he counted four men, armed. He shifted his gaze to the roof where he caught movement out of the corner of his eye. Running across the roof was a girl; the first thing he noticed was her bright red hair.

"Shit," Lee cursed realizing his plans for this place had just been squashed.

Lee followed the girl across the roof where she opened a skylight and dropped down inside. He scanned the windows for any sign of her; finally, he caught a glimpse of her in a room on the third floor.

"What the hell are you doing?"

She was leaned over a computer working, and instantly Lee knew exactly what this girl was up to. She was trying to steal data from Sheppard; exactly what he had did when he had taken three bullets to the back.

"Fucking hell," Lee said, setting the gun down on the roof beside him and unzipping the bag.

Lee pulled out the two forty-fives he had stolen and stuck them in his thigh holsters, then grabbed the other rifle he had that wasn't fitted for long range, and headed down the stairs. He made it to the street level and ran across the street and pressed himself up against the brick wall surrounding the building. The metal gate was locked tight and topped with several lines of razor wire, so climbing over wasn't an option. He walked around the side of the wall and surveyed his surroundings; he got a sprint going and jumped onto the wall on his left then shoved off of it, and did the same off the right wall then back to the left then over the wall on the right and into the outpost.

He landed on his feet and sprinted over behind some shipping crates. He peeked around the crates and counted the four men he had seen earlier. He stepped out, raising the rifle into firing position, and opened up on the four guards. No sooner had he killed the first two, an alarm began blaring. They were on to her. He took out the remaining two guards then ran for the door. Lee kicked the door open and was met by two more men. He raised the gun, but the first man grabbed the muzzle and jerked it to the side, tearing it loose from his grasp. Lee let go of the rifle and went to hand to hand combat against these two.

He landed a strong right hook into the first guy's face then ducked a blow from the second. He fired back with a jab to the second guy's gut which doubled him over and Lee slammed his knee up into his face. The first guy had recouped and swung nailing Lee in the side; Lee stumbled as the wind was knocked out of him. While Lee was stunned, the first guy made a grab for the rifle. Lee quickly spun and kicked, 'his foot connected with the man's head and the man's head connected with the wall, and with a sickening crack it squished as he fell to the floor dead.

The second guy was still on the ground recouping from his gut punch; he held his hands up in surrender as Lee turned to face him. Lee drew one of his pistols and fired, hitting the guy between the eyes. Lee started forward; he had to find this girl before they did.

Megan sat on the floor behind the desk as her device copied the hard drive as she was shot at from the doorway. She hadn't expected this place to be so guarded being one of the smaller outposts. She had done her research on which one of Sheppard's places to hit and this had been her best shot, now it looked like she wouldn't make it out. She knew the desk wouldn't hold up forever. Sooner or later, the bullets would eat a way through and find her, or destroy the computer before the files could be downloaded.

She also knew it was a mistake coming here without some kind of firearm. Sure, she had throwing knives, but if she rose up to throw one, she would be riddled with bullets. All in all, she was screwed. Then she heard gunshots from further down the hall and the fire was taken off of her. She took that chance to fight back. She grabbed two of her throwing knives and stood up. She slung them hitting two of the men in their necks, and then noticed another one of the men take a bullet to the head.

She grabbed her device and headed for the door — she would make a run for it. She noticed the gunfire had stopped; she pulled another knife from her hip bag and stepped out into the hall. On instinct, she slung the knife when she saw the guy walking up the hall towards her. Her knife found 'its target and buried itself into his shoulder, and she started down the hall.

"Goddamn it, I'm here to help you!"

She stopped, but as she did, she pulled another knife from her bag. She turned around to see the guy was still standing where he had been; he hadn't advanced on her or even raised his gun at her. He grabbed the hilt of the knife and pulled it out and blood began darkening the shoulder of his gray t-shirt.

"Who are you?"

"Someone who was going to blow this place to hell, until you decided to drop in. I have my own code," Lee said, before stopping and grabbing his shoulder. "I don't kill the innocent."

"I'm far from innocent," Megan said, noticing how pale he was becoming. "Greed demon."

"You're not..." Lee stopped as the pain in his shoulder intensified.

"Here," she said, digging into another of the bags on her and tossed him a small glass vial. "My knives are coated in an agent that causes severe pain; in a case like with you, I don't get a kill shot."

Lee caught the vial and looked at the green liquid in it.

"What's in it?"

"Just drink it, or you're going to be on the floor writhing in so much pain that you'll probably pull one of those guns on yourself," she explained. "If I was going to kill you, I'd just throw this knife at you right now."

Lee tossed the vial back to her.

"I'll take my chances."

"God, what are you a pride demon?"

"Yeah. Name is L..."

Lee fell forward unconscious. Megan sighed and knelt down beside him and rolled him over onto his back. She pushed his mouth open and poured the 'vial's contents in.

"I told you to drink it. Gotta say, you held out a lot longer than I expected, most people are on the floor within the first twenty seconds."

She stood up and looked around, she knew she couldn't carry him out of here and he most likely wouldn't wake up for a couple of hours and she couldn't just leave him here.

"This isn't going to be fun for you or me," she said, grabbing his wrists and dragging him down the hall.

She dragged him down to the elevator and hit the button. Once it arrived, she dragged him in and propped him up against the wall, and hit the first-floor button. Once the doors closed, she grabbed one of the guns from his thigh holster and got ready just in case there were guards left. The doors opened to a gory display straight from a horror movie. There were guards laying everywhere, riddled with bullet holes, their throats slit, head's crushed, and internals falling out.

"Damn. You're one badass motherfucker, huh?" She said, grabbing his wrists again and dragging him out.

After several minutes, she managed to get the front gate open then dragged Lee around the side of the building where her car was parked. She heaved him up into the passenger seat. After a moment to catch her breath, she climbed into the driver's seat and started the car.

"I hope I'm not taking a psycho back to my place," she said, looking over at Lee. "Strangely, I feel like I can trust you."

Sheppard

Oswald stood in front of the glass viewing window as they released three goats into the holding pen. The unsuspecting goats meandered around bleating, unaware they were being stalked in the dark by a man-made monster. One of the goats wondered a little too close to the dark corner of the room and was grabbed by a gray serpent and dragged into the darkness. The goat bleated several times before it was silenced, and a spray of blood came out of the darkness and splattered the concrete floor. Seconds later, the serpents emerged from the darkness and snatched the remaining two goats and pulled them back into the shadows.

"How is his implant responding?" Oswald asked, not taking his eyes from the scene before him.

"Full responsiveness in every test we have run."

"Good. I'm going in."

"Sir?"

"I want two goats," Oswald called as he shrugged off his jacket. "It's time we see if he's ready to be used in the field."

Oswald walked around to the entrance to the holding cell where he was led into a hall and was handed two leashes with goats on them. The door behind him closed sealing him in a small area, then the door before him opened and he walked out into the holding cell along with the two goats. The two serpents slowly emerged from the darkness followed by a young man.

"Owen?"

The young man stopped several feet in front of Oswald, his mouth — and all down the front of his shirt — were covered in drying goat blood.

"Take the goats."

Owen looked at the goats and the serpents grabbed them and began swallowing them whole.

"It's about time we let you out of your cage isn't it?" Oswald said, holding out a hand. "Come."

Owen mentally called his serpents back and they disappeared into his back, and he followed Oswald over to the door.

"Open the door," Oswald said, to lab workers on the other side.

The door rose and they stepped through. Oswald led Owen to another room where he opened a locker and pulled out some clothes and laid them down on the bed.

"Clean yourself up," Oswald said, pointing to the shower. "We have a lot to talk about."

Owen walked into the bathroom and turned on the shower. Oswald sat down on the bed and began his speech while Owen showered.

"There's an experiment, like you, who escaped a little while back. I'd like you to retrieve him. He's gone into the wind since our last attempt to retrieve him, but I figure a hunter like you will be able to find him."

Oswald heard the shower turn off and a moment later Owen stepped out of the bathroom with a towel wrapped around his waist. Owen walked over to Oswald who was holding the stack of clean clothes out to him.

"Where do I start looking?"

Tyler

Danny stepped outside blinded by the mid-morning sun. He shielded his eyes as he walked over to the van where Tyler, Aramis, and Simon were loading their stuff up.

"You look no worse for wear." Aramis said, after tossing a duffle bag into the back of the van. "How you feelin'?"

"Better than yesterday, but not as good as I'll feel tomorrow."

"What's tomorrow?" Simon asked.

"I was trying to be optimistic. Hopefully, by tomorrow, we can have dethroned Sheppard."

"High hopes, huh? You do know what we are going up against here right?"

"I spent seven years in that place. I know exactly what we are going up against," Danny turned to address them all as the rest of the group exited the house. "Let me go ahead and get this out there. This is most likely a one-way trip. If you want to back out, now is your chance."

The silence told Danny that they were all behind him on this mission and for that he was grateful. He was going to do everything in his power to make sure no one got hurt, but he couldn't make any promises; they were going into the depth of hell, so to speak.

"All right. Let's load up," Danny said, putting on his sunglasses and hopping up into the passenger seat.

"No word from your other guy?" Tyler asked Emma, as she climbed into the back of the van.

"No. Lee is... as stubborn as they come. He went after Sheppard; chances are we will catch up with him and, hopefully, he will have sorted out everything in his head and join us."

"So how long have you known him?" Tyler asked, sitting on the middle bench seat in front of Emma.

"We used to date. Things ended badly between us. He said, some things that hurt me and I, in my anger, cursed him, that's why he can't heal like you guys. Thing is, I don't know how to remove the curse I put on him."

"You can't go to like your coven or something and find out?"

"If I had a coven. One of the rules of being a witch is you don't have romantic relations with demons."

"But she did it twice," Logan said, sitting down beside Emma.

"I didn't mean to dig up your past. I was just a little concerned, him going off by himself like that, half-cocked and all."

"If there is one thing I have learned about Lee, it's that he never goes off half-cocked. He didn't eat, speak or hardly move after Soo was killed. I knew he was planning something. He's like a machine, calculating everything perfectly in his brain before acting."

"Let's go kick some Sheppard ass!" Bruce said, sitting down beside Tyler as Johnny started the van and pulled out onto the road and they began their long trip to Tucson.

Lee

Lee woke up and looked around at the strange surroundings, he tried to move but found his wrists handcuffed to the bed. The door to his right opened and the girl he had saved walked in and over to a small table on the far wall.

"Hey. Why am I locked up?"

"Because I still don't know if I can trust you."

"Where am I?"

"Here's how we will play this. You answer one of my questions and I'll answer one of yours. Deal?"

Lee shrugged and tried to lift his arms again, but found the cuffs didn't give him much leeway.

"Why were you there last night?"

"I've done told you this. I was going to blow that place to hell before you decided to meander in there. Where am I?"

"My place. How do I know you're not a spy for Oswald?"

"God. Did you not see all the fucking dead people? If I was a spy for Sheppard, why would I have slaughtered all his men?"

"Fair point. Your question?"

"Where are my clothes?" Lee asked, looking down at his bare torso; the only thing he was wearing was his underwear.

"Your shirt is in the trash, the rest I was washing. Frankly, they stunk. I did stitch your shoulder and give you a sponge bath. You're a demon, why don't you heal like one?"

"I was cursed. Ex-girlfriend troubles. Can you please unchain me now?"

Megan sighed and pulled the key from her pocket and unlocked the cuffs. Lee sat up on the edge of the bed rubbing his wrists as Megan leaned against the dresser in front of him. She felt fairly confident in her ability to tell a friend from an enemy and Lee felt nothing like an enemy.

"Any more questions?" Lee asked.

"Megan!"

They both jumped at the sudden yell and bang of the front door being forced open. Instinctively, Lee scanned the room for anything that he could use as a weapon if things got bad; there wasn't much to work with. The bedroom door flew open and a man entered.

"What the fuck is this?!" The man yelled staring Lee down.

"Tom, you have no business being here. I told you not to come back here."

"I have no business here?" He said, and grabbed Megan by the neck and slammed her back against the wall. "You fucking this guy behind my back?"

"Tom," Megan choked.

Lee grabbed a picture off the wall and slammed it down on top of the man's head. Lee knew instantly that the picture had been the wrong idea, his brain still foggy from whatever poison had been on Megan's knife. Tom dropped Megan, turned and kicked Lee in the chest sending him back and over the bed. Lee rolled to his hands and knees before Tom was on him again.

Tom grabbed Lee by his right arm and leg and threw him across the room and into the wall. Lee fell to the floor winded as Tom stomped over. Lee kicked out with all his might connecting with Tom's left knee. There was a sickening snap as Tom went down to his knees, his leg broken. Lee got to his feet and grabbed Tom's head and brought his knee up into his face several times. Lee let the man go and grabbed a large shard of glass from the floor and drove it into Tom's right eye.

Lee stood there for a moment as Tom lay on the floor in a pool of blood before he snapped out of it and walked over to Megan and helped her up to sit on the bed.

"You okay?" He asked, sitting down beside her.

"Yeah."

"Please... tell me..." Lee started.

She noticed his hands shaking and gently reached over and took them in hers.

"You did nothing wrong. He was a piece of shit. He's tried to rape me numerous times. He deserved everything he got."

"I need some air," Lee said, standing up.

"I have some beers in the fridge if you want one to help calm you down."

She looked over at Tom's body and began debating on the best way to dispose of it. She grabbed his hands and dragged him into the bathroom and rolled him into the tub. She then grabbed several towels and began cleaning up the blood. After a good ten minutes of cleaning, she ventured outside to find Lee sitting on the steps. The first thing she noticed was the bruise on his left shoulder where he had hit the wall when Tom threw him.

"Sorry, you got involved in my affairs."

"Killing those guys yesterday, it was nothing. I knew who they were, what they do. You say he was a bad guy, but how do I know that? I've become so fixated on revenge; I killed that guy without a second thought."

"Lee, all I can offer you is my word. He was a scumbag. I don't know what you want revenge for, but I want to help you. I can't explain it but I feel different around you like you are the first person I can trust in such a long time."

"You had me handcuffed."

"Just a precaution," Megan laughed.

"It's never easy. Killing. Even when it's the bad guys. There's something you feel here..." Lee hit his chest a couple of times. "It sits with you, eats away at you. It'll weigh you down if you let it, you have to accept the fact that some people will continue to harm others if you don't put them down."

Megan noticed the case of beers on the next step down and reached in to grab one. She had to go down to nearly the bottom of the box to get one. She felt inside and felt three left in the box besides the one she had taken, there had been eight in the box last night when she had gotten one.

"You've drunk four of these in the ten minutes it took me to get out here?"

"No. This is my first one."

"First one my ass. There were eight in here; now, there's three. What were you out here sculling them or something?"

"You got any food around here?"

"No. But we can go get something if you're not drunk off your ass."

"I can handle three beers."

"Four."

Lee held out the can he was holding that he had only taken one sip of. Lee stood up and set the can of beer on the railing that lined the porch.

"So where are we going?"

"You — inside to put some clothes on."

"Good point. I'll be out in a minute."

"Lee?"

Lee stopped in the doorway and turned back to Megan who was getting up off the step. He had to admit he found himself attracted to her, but he had just lost Soo and definitely wasn't ready for another relationship.

"What is it that you are fighting for?"

"My last girlfriend, Sheppard's men killed her. Sheppard wants something from us demons and he's willing to do anything to get it. I'm gonna be the one to put a bullet between his eyes. For Soo and what he did to me," Lee said, looking down at his feet. "Let me get dressed, and then we can talk over some food."

Megan nodded and Lee disappeared inside. Megan sighed, and picked up the box with the remaining cans of beer in it up and set it in a chair on the porch. Maybe she had figured out why she felt so comfortable around him, he was just like her, hellbent on making Oswald pay for what he had done to their lives and the ones they loved.

Megan drove them to a small burger joint where they ordered their food then parked in a quiet area and sat on the hood of the car to eat. Megan held out as long as she could before bombarding Lee with all the questions bubbling around in her mind since their last conversation on the porch.

"You said, Sheppard did something to you, what? If you don't mind me asking?"

"You know we demons aren't natural? We're not special, or superheroes. We're the product of a lab experiment gone wrong, years and years ago. Some escaped and bloodlines were crossed and now one in every ten thousand people born is a demon. We didn't originate in hell or ever work for Satan, as a lot of people like to believe. Two different kinds of demons. My parents were terrified of me, as is the case with most demon children. Guess who swooped in and whisked me away?"

"Hal Sheppard."

"Exactly. Took me to his lab where they poked and prodded and performed every kind of test under the sun to see what truly made me tick. Tortured me when I refused to use my abilities. Then one day, they just let me go. But they were always there watching, waiting for me to use my abilities, to see if I was what they needed. So, I used my abilities and I killed all the guys Sheppard had tailing me. I learned of more labs around the globe and what Sheppard was doing with others like me and made it my personal mission to shut him down. Then Hal died, and the devil himself came after me."

"Oswald."

"Oswald. I had a ragtag group, a family of sorts and Oswald came in and butchered them all, down to Bailey, a four-year-old girl. Butchered them all in an attempt to get me back to his lab. Their deaths are on me; their blood is on my hands. If I hadn't resisted, they might still be alive. He got me back to his lab anyway. Locked me away like some animal, drawing vial after vial of blood, shooting me up with stuff. I spent another four years in that hell before there was a massive outbreak. I think it was about ten of us that escaped. No clue who they are or where they went."

"Hell of a life."

"That's the short version," Lee said, taking a bite from his burger.

"Guess we all got our reasons for hating Sheppard. You mind if we go see a friend after we finish our food?"

"I'm your prisoner."

"He's someone who might be able to shed a little light on the whole Sheppard thing. Might be able to tell you some interesting things."

Lee finished his burger and leaned back against the windshield. Megan followed suit and lay back too.

"I'm taking it Sheppard fucked you over too?"

"That's one way of putting it. I was in that lab too, but I wasn't one of your ten. The females, once we reached maturity, we..."

"You don't have to. I get it."

"He said, it was to promote pure demon bloodlines again for his 'cure all' drug."

"It's a bullshit drug. Fucker is creating monsters, not a cure."

Megan chuckled.

"What?" Lee asked, confused.

"I think it's cute how much you cuss."

"You ain't seen me mad, that's when I say shit that doesn't make any sense. Emma made me mad once and I called her a fucking 'flubber assplug', what the hell is that?"

"You ready to go see Rain?"

"He sounds like a fun guy," Lee said, sitting.

"Wanna drive?" Megan said, holding out the keys.

"Hells yeah," Lee said, grabbing the keys and sliding off the hood.

Owen

Owen knelt down and examined the tracks left freshly in the dirt at a rundown house just outside of Los Angeles. He placed his right hand on the track and followed them with his eyes out onto the street where they continued for a few feet before disappearing. He stood up and began walking in the direction of the tracks. Owen scratched at the back of his head, where a small area of his hair was cut shorter just above his neck; he felt the small lump buried in there. He knew it was something Oswald had done to him, but at this point, he didn't care, he was out of that place and he would do whatever Oswald asked, as long as he got to stay out.

After following the road for nearly two hours, Owen found himself passing a small bar called 'Last Stop'. He debated on keeping to the road, but what could a five-minute stop hurt? He stepped off the road and crossed the dirt parking lot and went in. He was stared down by the whole ten customers and staff as he crossed the room to the bar.

"What can I get you?" A young woman asked him as he sat down.

"Water."

"Water it is," she said, grabbing a glass and filling it up at the sink. "Don't think I've ever had anyone come in asking for water before."

"There's a first time for everything," Owen said, then flinched, the voices in his head beginning.

"You all right?"

"Headache," Owen said, taking a sip of his water.

"Okay. I'll leave you to your water. You need anything just holler."

Owen put his head in his hands and sighed. The serpents were begging to be let out; they were hungry and would do whatever it took to get Owen to let them loose. He knew he couldn't hold them back forever; he was as much their slave as they were to him.

"Go," he whispered letting his grip on them go.

They instantly began to materialize out of his back.

"What the fuck?!"

Owen heard the shocked man's words then they were quickly followed by a crash, yelling and the spilling of bodily fluids. Owen simply sat at the bar sipping his water as the serpents tore their way through the people in the bar. It took them all of two minutes to kill off all ten people. Owen turned on his stool to face the carnage behind him, the scene was something straight out of a horror flick, blood and body parts were strewn everywhere and his serpents gobbling them up.

Owen sighed and stood up as his serpents returned to him and dissipated. He had to admit after they fed, he did feel more powerful and as he stepped out of the bar he felt as if he could almost see the trail of the car he was after. He started back down the road on his search for the demon Oswald was so hellbent on getting back.

Taka

Taka wasn't too sure what to expect from his meeting with the vampire elders, he paced the room waiting for them. Convincing them to make a stand against Sheppard and the witches' coven wouldn't be that hard; the hard part would be getting them to trust the last three remaining warlocks. Taka sighed and sat down in one of the chairs in the living room looking room they had him waiting in. No sooner had he sat down when the door opened and two vampires entered followed by a young boy.

"You said, you had urgent matters to discuss with us," the first of the vampires said, taking a seat.

"I do. It involves Oswald Sheppard and Dana."

"I'm listening."

"Dana killed all my warlocks. Save me, my brother and Michael. Put spells over Judah and Michael and forced me to watch as she and her witches slaughtered every one of my men. All in a ruse to get us to play along nicely while she buddied up with Sheppard. Oswald is planning something, and it involves all of us."

"You don't know what he is planning?" The second vampire asked.

"A war, between all species. We sided with the witches'

coven because they were to help us stop Sheppard before this war could start, seems Dana is deeper in Sheppard's pocket than I had imagined."

"So it would seem. Jacoby, go and gather the remaining elders. Seems we can no longer ride in the dark, war is on our horizon."

The boy nodded and left the room.

"It may not come as any consolation, it sure didn't with me, but I have word from an old friend that there is a ragtag band of demons out to shut Sheppard down."

"Demons," the vampire said, with a laugh. "The by-product of a man-made experiment gone wrong. Guess we can't afford to be picky in such a situation. Rally what you can and meet me in two days."

"Thank you," Taka said, bowing and turning to leave the room.

"Taka. Be sure and let your recruits know they will be tested. A single drop of blood will tell Jacoby all he needs to know. We can't afford any traitors."

Taka nodded and left. The vampire's powers never ceased to amaze him. How a single drop of blood could play in their heads the whole lifetime of a person in seconds, no wonder the cops secretly used vampires in their investigations.

"Taka."

Taka stopped to face a young female vampire coming around the side of the building.

"I know you are recruiting people for this war with Sheppard. Can you find my brother? His name is Nathan," she said, handing Taka a photo. "Please, he would be invaluable to your cause."

"I'll see what I can do. I have a guy who is good at tracking."

"Thank you."

Taka looked down at the photo again and by the time he looked back up the girl was gone, nowhere to be seen.

Lee

Margret paced the room, she knew in her heart what she and Drew were about to do wasn't right, but then again neither was her baby. The babe lay in the crib crying, small and malnourished, death already closing in on him. Drew descended the stairs, his shirt damp in several places.

"What if we're wrong?" Margret said, blocking Drew's path to the baby. "What if he isn't like the other?"

"You saw the other one. We're not taking the risk."

"His name was Noah."

"I told you not to name them. It may be hard but it's the right thing to do. We can't raise no freak."

Drew moved past Margret and picked up the baby and began to head back upstairs as the baby squalled in his arms. Margret sat down on the couch and buried her head in her hands crying. The baby's crying abruptly stopped and Margret sobbed even more knowing that Drew had plunged the babe into the tub and was holding it under the water.

The front door burst open and several men in tactical uniforms rushed in. Margret looked up only to be hit in the head with a bullet. Two of the men searched the first floor while two more headed upstairs. Hal Sheppard walked through the door and looked around. There was another gunshot from upstairs then silence.

"We've got the two children up here. One deceased, the other possibly deceased," a man said, over the radio.

A moment passed then Hal heard crying.

"The second target is alive."

The men from upstairs descended the stairs the first carrying the baby, which he handed off to Hal. Hal cradled the child pulling the towel tighter around 'its cold wet body.

"You're safe now little one."

Lee snapped awake, then breathed a sigh of relief and sat back in the passenger seat of the car.

"You okay?" Megan asked, looking over at him.

"Bad dream."

"Want to talk about it?"

"Not particularly," Lee said, sitting up in the seat. "I haven't dreamed about my parents in a long time. Last time I did, it was right before some bad shit went down."

"We'll let's hope no bad shit is coming our way."

"They were trying to kill me."

"Your parents?"

"I had a brother, they did kill him. My dad was drowning me when Hal and his men saved me."

"Hal Sheppard?"

"He saved me to lock me away in another hell, but he saved me all the same. It's what one in a million chance you'll be born a demon, and my parents had two. The luck huh?"

Megan pulled off the road and onto a small dirt road leading off into the woods. She followed the road for a while before it opened up into a large field with a house sitting in the middle of it. She pulled the car to a stop beside another car and turned the ignition off.

"Ready?" Megan asked, opening her door.

Lee opened his door and stepped out. He looked the house over as they made their way to the porch. Nothing looked out of the ordinary, no indication that a demon lived here. Megan knocked on the door while Lee looked at a deer skull on a small table near the door.

"Shot that one a few weeks ago."

They both turned at the voice behind them. Walking up was a man in his early thirties carrying a line with several fish on it.

"I hope you guys like fish."

Danny

Danny flipped through the radio stations while Bruce, Aramis, and Logan all argued about which weapon was best to hunt with. Danny finally found something worth listening to and sat back in the seat and glanced over at Johnny behind the wheel.

"Need me to drive for a while?" Danny asked.

"Sorry, but I don't trust anyone else behind the wheel."

"Narcissistic much?"

"Let's just call it an extra precaution. Let's not resort to name calling, save that for me and Bruce."

"You two are crazy," Danny laughed.

"It's harmless fun, we both know we're just screwing around. Unlike when he and that new guy got into it, that shit was real. I was scared for that guy, I thought Bruce was going to lose his shit again and tear him apart."

"Yeah, I wish everyone would just leave him alone about his orientation."

"It doesn't bother me. He's gay, I don't care."

"He's bi, and our lives are hard enough without nitpicking all the little shit."

"I ag..."

Before Johnny could finish his response, the van was

struck from the left side and sent rolling off the road. The van flipped three times before coming to a stop on its right side. Danny's ears were ringing and his head felt like it was inside a bubble. He shook off the feeling and unbuckled himself and climbed out through the broken windshield. Danny stumbled to his feet and noticed the figure walking towards them.

Danny noticed something else as the figure was approaching; it had two serpents hovering over its shoulders. Last Danny had heard, he was the last archdemon.

"What the hell happened?" Johnny said, climbing out the way Danny had gotten out and walked over beside Danny. "The fuck?"

"Get the others out of here," Danny said, starting towards the approaching figure.

"Danny! Come with me now and your friends don't have to die!"

Danny stopped as did the figure. Danny slowly let out his breath then grabbed the two pistols he had tucked in the waistband of his pants and fired several shots at the stranger. His serpents immediately intercepted the bullets then shot forward towards Danny. Danny ducked and rolled to the right to dodge the serpents' attacks. He got to his feet and fired several more rounds at his attacker as he ran to get a little more distance between them, but he wasn't quick enough.

One of the serpents grabbed his ankle and brought him down to the ground where he lost one of his pistols as it began dragging him back towards its host. Danny fired blindly behind him as he was being dragged back. After he fired off the third shot, he felt sharp pains in his arm, realizing the second serpent had grabbed his arm in its mouth. Danny was only a few feet from his attacker when he heard more gunfire from further away.

Danny silently cursed his companions. He had told Johnny to get them out of here. Apparently, one of the group's bullets had hit home in the attacker because for a moment the serpents released their grip on Danny and that's when Danny made his move. Danny rolled over onto his back and raised his gun and fired several more rounds into the guy. The man stumbled back a few steps then looked at Danny and smirked.

The bullets that had hit him were being pushed out and the wounds healing almost instantly. The man walked over to Danny and grabbed him by the neck and lifted him up. Danny tried to reach his pocket where he had an extra clip for his pistol, but one of the serpents grabbed his arm and held it firmly.

"This could have been easy. But you chose the hard way."

Danny noticed movement out of the corner of his eye. He then noticed it was Simon running over, sword pulled back at the ready.

"No," Danny tried to yell, but his lack of breath didn't allow more than a whisper.

The stranger noticed the approaching threat and reacted accordingly. The second serpent shot forward faster than Simon could swing and buried itself into his chest. Simon dropped the blade and looked up at Danny with a look of pure shock on his face before the serpent drew back bringing with it, Simon's heart in its jaws. Simon dropped to his knees placing his hands over the gaping hole in his chest.

"No!" Aramis yelled fighting against Bruce and Tyler who were holding him back.

Danny remembered the small pocket knife he had in his left pocket and made a grab for it while the serpent was occupied devouring Simon's heart. He brought it out and flipped it open. He slashed the man's arm holding him and Danny was dropped. Danny quickly landed on his feet and brought the knife up into the man's side, which caused enough pain for the serpent holding his right arm to let go. Danny pulled the blade free and slung it upwards cutting the man across the face.

If he could cause the man enough pain his serpents would be forced back within him to heal his wounds. Danny went for one final blow and brought the knife down into the man's chest as he was shielding his face. After planting the knife, Danny made a mad sprint for the group.

"Light him up!" Johnny yelled once Danny was clear.

Danny reached the group as the man was brought down in a hail of gunfire. As Danny had expected, his serpents had vanished back inside him to heal his wounds, but that wouldn't take long — they needed to make their escape now.

"We can't take it all. Just grab what you can carry and let's go," Johnny said, picking up a couple of bags of their supplies.

Johnny tossed Danny another pair of pistols and a backpack of supplies.

"Don't lose those. They were my fathers," Johnny said, shouldering his bag.

Danny pulled the backpack on and shoved the pistols into his waistband and they started off across the field, continuing their journey to Tucson and away from this other archdemon.

The Boy

Thunder shook the thin pane windows of the Martin farmhouse. Maggie had just finished setting the table for Kyle and herself. The downpour had been steady for the past hour and had caused them to have to close up shop early. Maggie stood at the kitchen sink filling a pitcher of water when she noticed someone run into the barn.

"Kyle!" She called walking over to the table with the water.

"I'm coming," he said, walking in.

"Someone just ran into the barn."

Kyle turned and grabbed his shotgun from a shelf above the fireplace and checked to make sure it was loaded. Maggie gently put her hand on the barrel and lowered it.

"It looked like a child."

"Just in case," Kyle said, heading for the door.

Maggie hesitated then followed him out the door. They crossed the backyard to the barn and Kyle opened the door.

"Someone in here?"

Maggie slowly made her way into the barn and looked around. She noticed what Kyle hadn't: small footprints. She gently nudged Kyle and pointed to the trail.

"Put that away," Maggie whispered as she began to

make her way to the end of the trail.

She made it to the last stall and looked over the door. Cowering in the back corner was a small boy.

"It's okay," she said, opening the stall door. "No one here is going to hurt you."

The boy remained cowering in the corner. Maggie noticed the tattered clothes he was wearing and knew he had been on the run for some time. She slowly reached her hand out.

"It's okay child. Let's get you inside where it's warm. You'll catch a cold out here in those wet clothes."

After a few minutes, the boy slowly came forward and took her hand. Maggie brushed some hair out of his face and gave him a warm smile. She guessed he was about twelve, brown eyes and brown hair. She led him into the house and got him a towel to wrap in while she put his shirt and jeans in the dryer.

"Sit down. You hungry?"

Maggie fixed another bowl of soup and brought it over to the boy who began digging into it like he hadn't eaten in ages.

"After you eat, we can get you cleaned up. A nice hot shower."

"What are you on the run from boy?"

"Kyle, let the boy eat. Poor kid is all skin and bones. You can play your twenty questions later."

The boy turned his bowl up and drained every remaining drop of soup then set it down, then pointed at the bowl.

"You can have more," Maggie said, picking up the bowl and heading back to the pot of soup on the stove.

She brought back another bowl full and the boy greedily

set into it. After several more bowls, Maggie showed the boy to the bathroom where she turned on the shower for him.

"You get cleaned up and I'll go check on your clothes. There are towels and rags in the closet there," she pointed to a door on the far side of the bathroom. "There are soap and shampoo in there, I'll lay your clothes on the sink here."

Maggie left and the boy dropped the towel to the floor and got in the shower. He let the warm water warm his skin, let it wash over his hair and face. He washed then sat down and pulled his knees up to his chest and just let the water wash over him. As much as he might want it to, he knew this couldn't last, nothing good ever lasted long. He rested his chin on his knee, thinking about the life he had left behind, everything that had led him to this point and what he was.

He knew he had to leave; he couldn't stay and risk these people getting hurt because of him. No one was going to die because of him, not again.

Danny

After a couple of hours walking, the rain had started; they had found a small motor inn and rented a room. Aramis was on the bed, not speaking still in shock after seeing his best friend killed. Tyler and Bruce were sitting at the small table playing cards, while Kyler and Johnny were out scoping the area out and Emma and Logan were out getting food. Danny dropped his backpack onto the floor and went into the bathroom.

He was feeling Aramis' pain; hell, he couldn't help but feel Simon's death was his fault. Simon had been trying to save him after all, so wasn't he to blame? Danny locked the door and pulled his shirt off and tossed it to the floor and walked over to the sink and turned it on. He leaned on the sink waiting on the water to warm up and closed his eyes.

He sighed looking up at his reflection in the mirror. This was why he never worked in groups, he got attached and he ended up not being able to protect them. He filled his hands with water and tossed it up onto his face. He splashed his face with water several more times, and then winced in pain. He took a few steps back so he could see his stomach in the mirror and the purple bruising returning where he had been stabbed.

Whatever this was, it was definitely taking its toll on him, and apparently, Emma hadn't been able to get rid of it. He noticed the same bruising showing up on his neck again; he could hide his stomach, but not his neck. Danny jumped when there was a knock on the door.

"You all right?" Tyler asked.

"Yeah, I'll be out in a minute."

Danny looked at his stomach in the mirror one more time before picking up his shirt and pulling it back on. Luckily, his neck wasn't very noticeable yet, but it soon would be.

Oswald

Dana had made the long drive to Tucson upon Oswald's request. She knew exactly what he was wanting, an update on the progress she had made with the warlocks and their war plans. She rode the elevator down for what seemed like forever after going through four security checkpoints. Once the elevator finally stopped, she stepped out into a large open room where she faced a thirty-foot long glass wall looking out at a forest like area. Dana walked over to the glass and looked out at the trees and vines that filled the room.

"It's real. No fancy technology there, aside from what it takes to keep it up and going," Oswald said, walking up beside her.

"How is this possible? We're what, a hundred metres underground?"

"Three hundred. It takes lots of technological advances. Artificial sunlight and having the elements just right. It's not an easy feat."

"And it's just for looks?"

"What do you take me for a botanist?" Oswald chuckled. "There are things living in there that you couldn't even imagine in your worst nightmares. They're not why you are here."

Oswald led Dana out of the large open room and down a hall to his office. Dana took a seat in one of the large chairs set in front of the desk while Oswald poured them both a glass of bourbon. Oswald handed Dana her glass then took his seat behind his desk.

"So how did things go with Taka?"

"As planned. He is meeting with the vampires as we speak. They, in turn, will reach out to the demons. War will then be on the horizon once the other races hear of alliances forming. Then you have your chance to swoop in as the savior."

"Perfect. We will finally be able to rid ourselves of the unnecessary species that provide a drain on our resources; the human, namely."

"And this demon you want, why is he so important?"

"Danny," Oswald said, then took a sip of his drink. "Danny is special. You have any idea how many failed attempts we have had at creating more like him?"

Oswald opened a drawer on his desk and pulled out a file about eight inches thick and slid it across the desk to Dana.

"Nine hundred and sixty-two failures. Two successes. While Owen is considered a success, he is unpredictable; he lacks the strength Danny has shown. Everything we threw at Danny, he overcame. Polio, meningitis, cancer — nothing could stop him."

"Basically, your ace in the hole got away?"

"In a manner. He's resilient. Every attempt to capture him has ended badly for me; I've lost over two hundred men to him."

"Sounds like a tough cookie. You didn't call me here to talk about your failures though."

"Indeed. I'd like you and your witches to move in on the lycans. Let's make the vampires' first move without them even knowing they have made it."

"As you wish," Dana said, and stood to leave.

"Dana. Let's loosen Taka's leash a little, see what kind of trouble he starts on his own."

Dana nodded and left the room. Oswald looked at the file he had slid across the desk to Dana — all the failures it contained. He knew his plans were useless without Danny in his possession. Without Danny, all he would be doing was bringing about an Armageddon of sorts instead of an ideal world. He had to have Danny back, no matter the costs.

Danny

"How long has this been back?" Emma asked, gently touching Danny's stomach. "I thought I got it out of you."

"I noticed it earlier."

"Shit. I'm gonna have to try and cleanse you again, the difficult way this time."

"Difficult sounds painful."

"Yeah. Very. I'm going to have to send Logan for some supplies," she said, opening the bathroom door.

They were greeted by the rest of the group, waiting to hear about what the two of them were doing in the bathroom together. Emma walked over to the bed Aramis wasn't on and patted it.

"Shirt off and lie down on your stomach."

Danny sighed then pulled his shirt off and walked over to the bed and lay down. Emma grabbed her bag and pulled out a pad and pen and began writing down all she needed then tossed the pad to Logan.

"Quickly as you can."

"I thought you fixed him before?" Bruce said.

"I guess not. I'm gonna need a lot of help this time. Tyler, get me two bowls or whatever you can find of hot water. Johnny, some rags from the bathroom."

Emma pulled a small tin box from her bag and took out a syringe and bottle. She stuck the syringe into the bottle and drew some of the liquid out.

"Okay, Danny, this is going to make you feel funny. I'm trying to make this as painless as I can," she said, sticking the needle into the side of his neck. "That should have kicked in really good by the time Logan gets back. Just relax."

Tyler returned with two receptacles of hot water and Johnny with a stack of rags. Emma gently brushed hair out of Danny's face and saw he was already out. She pushed the waistband of his pants down a little then dipped one of the rags in the water and began wiping over Danny's lower back.

"How much do you guys know about arch demons?" Emma asked, wiping over Danny's back.

"Not much," Johnny said.

"Arch demons have a sort of hidden organ. It's right around here," Emma touched Danny's back just above his left hip. "It's kind of like a second liver. It lies dormant most of the time but, given the right jolt, we can jumpstart it and hopefully it will help us cleanse his blood of this curse."

"I don't know about y'all, but an inch of Danny's butt crack is more of Danny's ass than I need to see."

"I've got to be able to get to the organ," Emma said, as the door opened and Logan walked in with a bag.

Logan brought the bag over to Emma and set it on the bed beside Danny. Emma set about combining some of the items into a thin paste then drew them up into a syringe. She combined the remaining items into a green liquid and filled another syringe.

"Tyler, you are my automatic volunteer. You said, you two are brothers; we're going to need you to be our donor for his blood transfusion. Don't wander off."

Emma picked up the first syringe then felt around in the area she knew the organ to be. Once satisfied she had found the right spot, she slowly inserted the syringe into Danny's back. She kept the needle going in slowly; she knew if he jerked or moved, she had probably hit a nerve, and if he moved too much, she could miss the organ entirely and cause Danny more trouble than he was in now.

She felt the needle pierce the organ and breathed a sigh of relief. One down, one to go. She slowly pushed the plunger down on the syringe injecting the mixture she had made. Once the syringe was empty, she slowly pulled it out and wiped the area with a clean wet rag.

"Logan, you want to go ahead and start prepping Tyler?"

"Sure."

Tyler sat down in a chair beside the bed and let Logan take his arm and feel for a vein in the bend of his elbow. Logan found a vein and cleaned the area then stuck the needle in and got everything ready with some sort of bottle. Emma managed to get the second syringe in and injected the second mixture without any problems.

"Johnny and Bruce, I need him turned over onto his back. Gently."

Johnny and Bruce got Danny turned over onto his back and Logan hooked Danny up to the other end of the weird transfusion bottle.

"So why does he need blood?" Bruce asked, sitting down on the edge of the bed.

"Jumpstarting this other organ is going to cause him to lose a lot of blood. This kind of curse attacks the blood, and while all of his blood isn't contaminated, a lot is, and it's going to be sent to this 'second liver' so to speak where it will be destroyed. The contamination, the blood, all of it. It's a complicated process, but I've seen it before."

The conversation stopped as gunshots were heard outside. Johnny and Bruce grabbed their weapons and got ready. Two more pistol shots, closer this time. Logan approached the door and nodded to Johnny. Johnny opened the door and Logan stepped out scanning the area. He saw two people across the parking lot, along with six men closing in on them in tactical armor. Logan recognized the guy, but not the girl he was with.

"Lee!"

Lee turned and saw Logan and a look of relief came over him.

"Go," Lee said, pushing the girl forward towards the room where Logan was.

Logan provided cover fire as the girl and Lee ran for the room. Johnny shut the door and bolted it before several bullets tore through it.

"Move further in," Johnny said, as bullets shattered the window.

"We aren't going to be able to stay here. They got this big motherfucker with them," Lee said, reloading his gun.

"We can't leave. Danny is in no condition to go anywhere," Johnny explained.

Lee looked over at the bed where Danny was lying and Emma crouched down beside it. She had made another one of her protective shields around herself, the bed and a guy in a chair beside the bed. The door was kicked open and Butch stepped in. He grabbed Johnny's gun as he raised it and twisted it free of Johnny's hands then bashed Johnny across the face with it. Bruce put two shots into Butch's chest, but it didn't seem to faze him. Butch grabbed Bruce's wrist and snapped it then slung Bruce out of the way.

Lee landed several hits, but nothing seemed to hurt this guy; Butch grabbed Lee and slammed his head up against the wall, he began applying more and more pressure trying to crush Lee's head. There was sickening tearing sound and Butch's grip on Lee's head let up. Lee crumpled to the floor and looked up to see Butch's body drop to its knees, 'its head gone. Lee saw the guy who had been lying on the bed under Emma's shield standing there, two smoky serpents hovering around him, one of them swallowing Butch's head.

"Danny, stop. You're not strong enough yet," Emma said, putting a hand on his shoulder.

Danny shrugged her hand off his shoulder and headed for the door. He stepped outside to be greeted by the five other men in their tactical armor. Danny nodded and his serpents shot forward grabbing the closest man by an arm and a leg and tearing him in half. One of the serpents grabbed the next man by the head and slung him across the parking lot and into the side of a parked car. Danny picked up one of the men's dropped rifles and began helping his serpents pick the men off one by one.

Emma knelt down beside Lee and looked at his head and the black eye already setting in. After making sure he was okay, Emma went to the door. She saw Danny on his knees in the middle of the parking lot. The rain had started again drenching her as she walked over to him. She knew he had exerted himself too much after what she had just done to him. She knelt down beside him.

"What did you do to me?"

"It's complicated."

"I've never had that much control over them. I let them loose and they do their own thing, but this time, it was like I pictured what I wanted in my head and they did it."

"You got a lot to learn, bud. You've barely scratched the surface of what you can do."

"How do you know so much about this stuff?"

"My father was an archdemon. It's kind of the reason I'm not a part of the witches' coven, one of many reasons. Come on, we need to get out of here before the po-po shows up."

She helped Danny to his feet then looked at his belly where the bruising had been, it was gone.

"Don't hate me, but it was the only way to save you, you're going to have to let them feed more often now."

"I had the feeling you were going to tell me something like that."

Griffin

Test subject one
March, 10
The virus was injected directly into living flesh;
the subject is expected to begin mutation within
24 to 48 hours.

Griffin woke up lying on an exam table in nothing but his underwear, with a killer headache, and he couldn't move. He could hear a man and woman talking somewhere in the room.

"Blood work is clean. Slight anomaly in the CT scan. What did you get from the physical?" The male voice said.

"He is covered in bruises. His thigh has a wound, most likely the cause of his infection. The stomach is a bit hard..." He felt cold gloved hands press on his belly. "I don't think it's from the Necrophagous virus."

What the hell is a Necrophagous virus? What were these people doing to me? What were they talking about and what did it have to do with me?

"We can't be risky," the man said.

"Right. Pull what you can from his memories and put him in stasis."

"What about the girl and the other boy?" The man asked.

"I want the girl in T-Sector. Wipe the smaller boy's memory and take him home."

"Why bother? They'll all be dead soon enough."

Griffin tried to look around but the bright lights above him caused him to only see bright glaring light. He tried to speak, but found himself incapable.

"He's awake."

Griffin felt a sharp pain in his right arm and as his vision cleared a little, he saw the woman pull a needle out. Her face became blurry and his eyes heavy — soon, he was out again.

When Griffin came to, all he could hear was the howling wind. His body was cold. He forced his eyes open and looked around. He found his face was covered by a thin cloth and he was lying on something hard and was being drug. Cold snow brushed his arms and legs. He gave one jolt of his hips and rolled off the platform.

He went face first into the freezing snow then scrambled to his feet and threw the cloth off his head.

"Hey, calm down. We're not going to hurt you," an Asian boy that looked about twenty said. "We're taking you to our place."

Griffin looked at the other two men who had been dragging him. They were older; one had a beard painted white by the snow, the other had a short beard. They all wore heavy coats and goggles, hoods and thick cloths over their nose and mouths. The last thing he noticed were the guns strapped to their hips.

"What are the guns for?"

"I'm Ken. This is Paul and Tom. We have to get you inside where it's warm. The way you're dressed you'll freeze to death in under ten minutes."

Griffin looked down at his blue jeans and t-shirt then back to the guns on their hips. He was freezing and had no other options.

"Do you know where my brother is?"

"We only found you," Ken said.

Griffin followed them. The snow was up to his shins and his pants legs were becoming heavy and soaking wet. His shoes felt like lead and his feet ached with every step. Ken tied the cloth that had been over his head earlier over his mouth and nose.

"Keep your head down. The wind is picking up."

Their home was what looked like an arctic research facility; it was a one-story building covering the horizon as they mounted a large snow cap. The gray building was dull looking on the white tundra. Off to the right side of the building was a shed.

"Welcome home," Ken said, and started towards the building.

Inside, it was warm. A haven from the frigid environment they had just left. The first room was large and the wall to the left of the entrance was lined with thick coats and boots.

"Who is this?" A young girl asked, walking out of a room packed with computer screens.

"New guy. Found him during the run," Paul said.

She eyed Griffin several times. Her skin was a very light brown. She was very pretty. She wore a pink shirt and a tan jacket with blue jeans.

"Jill," She said, thrusting her hand out.

Griffin took her hand, but his mouth seemed to be filled

with cotton. She smiled then released his hand.

"Griffin," He blurted before she turned away.

"Nice to meet you, Griffin. If you'll follow me, I'll get you to your room and get you some dry clothes. You must be freezing."

She started down the hall then took a right then followed another hall and took a left and about halfway down this hall stopped and opened a door.

"Here's your room. I'll be right back with some fresh clothes."

She disappeared down the hall as he went into the room and looked around. It was nice. There was a full-size bed, a desk with a computer on it and a dresser with a television on it. The closet was at the foot of the bed and had mirrored doors. Griffin walked over to them and looked at himself.

What's going on? How did I get here? Why am I having trouble remembering anything before being dragged through the snow? A million questions flowed through his mind as he stood there staring into his own eyes.

"Here you go," Jill said, handing him a stack of clothes. "Admiring ourselves, are we?"

"I do look good," he said, smiling. "I can't remember much. I remember some things, but not much. I have to find my brother and Rachel."

"Who is Rachel?"

Griffin turned back to look at himself in the mirror again, but jumped back and fell onto the bed. His eyes were glowing an orange-yellow. Jill looked at him shocked and knelt down by the bed.

"You okay?" She asked.

"Yeah." he said, looking at his reflection again, the

glowing eyes now gone.

"Cloths, bed," she said, pointing out each one. "Dinner's at seven."

She started for the door.

"Thank you."

Griffin changed and lay down on the bed. As soon as his head hit the pillow, he was out. It wasn't a peaceful sleep though, he kept seeing Rachel. Kept having images of small parasites swimming around in his blood infecting all of his blood cells. This continued until he was awakened by Jill.

The dining hall was a large room with three tables. There were eight people in the room around the tables. There were five men and three women. Griffin sat down beside Jill as another woman set steaming plates of food down in front of them.

"This is Amy. Amy, this is Griffin."

"You remind me of my son," she said, with a bit of sadness. "You have his smile."

"Her son passed away last month," Jill said, as Amy walked away.

"How?"

"I'll explain after dinner. It's easier shown than said. Things may seem a little weird."

After dinner, they went down several other long halls and into a small room big enough for two. There were two sets of walls. The normal building walls then set a foot away from that was the glass room they stood in. The steel door in front of them had a biohazard sticker in the center of it below the round window. A fine mist began spraying down on them, Griffin looked around confused.

"It's okay. It's just sterilizing us," she explained.

The mist stopped and the door made a clicking sound and released with a loud hiss. The next room was also white tiled like the other rooms and lined with tables full of lab equipment. On the adjacent wall was a glassed-off section with an exam table inside. A sheet covered an object lying on it.

"What is this place?"

"Welcome to ground zero. This is where the first one was found. It was discovered by one of our team. He's dead now," she explained.

"It?"

She opened the door to the glassed-off room and went inside. She walked over to the table and pulled the sheet back. Underneath was a boy, he looked about twelve.

"This is Amy's son. He was attacked while outside. You'll notice the lumps in his stomach," she pointed out two places where the boy's stomach lumped out. "It attacks its host, kills them and plants its eggs in the stomach. We think the eggs are still growing inside him."

"How could you find out?" Griffin asked, not really believing any of this.

"Cut him open. We've been afraid to. But I think we would rather face it as a newborn opposed to fully-grown. Grown they are nearly impossible to kill."

She walked over to another slab and pulled the sheet back. Beneath it was what looked like a man. The face was distorted and split from the nose down to the bottom of the neck, small teeth lined each side of the opening. Veins stood out in his skin and his arms were tucked in tightly against his sides and covered with a thin yellowish skin. His stomach was ripped open and his insides were browning with decay.

Spider-like arms protruded from his back and were tipped with black razor-sharp talons.

"What the fuck is that?" Griffin said, taking a few steps closer. "Is it dead?"

"Yeah. Gates killed it a week ago. This is what we have been facing and what killed Luke, the boy. We have seen how they operate. These arms here," she pointed to the spider-like arms. "Grab you and pull you towards the mouth," she motioned at the opening in its neck. "The stomach is ripped open because there's a projecting tube that plants the eggs."

"Bullshit! What am I on some kind of TV show? Where are the cameras?"

"Griffin, this is all real. This is why I said, I wanted to show you."

There was a squishing sound then cracking. Silence. They both turned around to look at Luke.

"I want out of here," Griffin said.

More squishing and cracking. This time the boy's stomach moved. Up and then back down.

"Get. The. Door. Open. Now."

More noises. This time, the boy's stomach went up and stayed up. The shape slowly moved up into his chest causing the skin to stretch. There was a loud cracking sound then gurgling as the boy's neck stretched and two clawed fingers protruded from his mouth. Two more fingers came out and grabbed the top of his mouth. Slowly, the hands began pushing the boy's jaws apart. There was a cracking as the boy's bones snapped and his bottom jaw fell limply onto his chest as the creature forced its way out.

Jill fumbled with the door lock. The creature squeezed

its way out of the boy's stretched mouth and fell onto the floor.

"It's out. Get the door open."

She typed on the keyboard and the door locks released. The sound caught the thing's interest. Its clawed hand came out from the other side of the table.

"Get the door open," Griffin said.

The creature's head peered around; its head was round and had to rows of eyes, each row consisting of three eyes. 'Its bottom jaw opened and split down the center revealing more jagged teeth.

Jill opened the door and pulled Griffin through and slammed it shut. The creature pounded on the three-inch steel door as the mist sprayed down on them again.

"What… the fuck was that?!"

She pulled a radio from her pocket and held it close to her mouth.

"Gates."

"Go for Gates."

"We have a big problem. Is the morgue locked down?"

There were a few moments of silence before he came back. The silence let them know they could expect the worst.

"Amy and Reeves are down there. What's going on?"

"Get them out of there now!" She said, shoving the radio into her pocket and started running down the hall.

Griffin broke into a run be she was too fast. No matter how hard he tried, he couldn't keep up. She threw open the door to the security room and went in. She walked over to a set of monitors and looked at the morgue. Griffin walked in out of breath and stood beside her. On the screen, Amy was crawling across the floor everything from her waist down missing.

"Where's Reeves?" Jill asked the man sitting at the monitors.

"He left right before all this," the man said.

"Damn it! Find him."

Griffin had finally caught his breath as he watched her pull out the radio again.

"Gates. Check the locks on the morgue then I want every able body to search for Reeves."

"Solid copy."

Jill grabbed Griffin's shoulder and turned him towards the door. She walked him to the door then turned back around to face the man in the security room.

"Lock the door behind us. Code yellow."

She shut the door behind them and an alarm began going off. Griffin jumped at the sound of it but Jill grabbed his hand and led him to another room down another hall. She stopped at the door and entered a code onto the door lock. The lock clicked and she pushed the door open. Shoving him into the pitch-black room she closed the door.

"I don't like the dark," Griffin said.

There was a click then mechanical buzzing as the overhead lights came to life revealing shelves of guns.

"Welcome to the armory. Get something to fight with. We have to find Reeves before he infects anyone else," she said, picking up a rifle.

Griffin touched one of the guns hanging on the shelf in front of him, felt the cold steel. He grabbed one of the rifles and held it at firing position.

"Be sure you get a gun that is comfortable. The last thing you want is to fire a gun that doesn't fit you. Here."

She tossed him a harness with a pistol in it. She wrapped hers around her thigh and he did the same. She pulled a wooden box out from under the shelf and opened it. She tossed him six clips then grabbed a chest harness from another box. It was made of two leather straps that went on your shoulder like a backpack, but crossed on the back. On the left shoulder, it held a knife, and on the straps going down each side, it had slots to hold the magazines.

"Not only does it make you look sexy, but you're ready to kick some ass," she said, pulling on her harness.

"You think those things are going to get out?" Griffin asked.

"Even if they don't get out, we still have to find Reeves, who is most likely infected. I'd rather have it and not need it than need it and not have it."

"True."

"Last touches."

She crossed the room and opened a closet set into the far wall. She tossed him a tan coat, a scarf, and a gas mask. Griffin pulled on the coat and wrapped the scarf around his neck and over his mouth and nose as Ken had shown him earlier.

"What's this for?" Griffin asked, holding up the mask.

"In about," she checked her watch. "Five minutes the place is going to be purged. Everyone has been evacuated into the safe house."

"Purged?" He asked, not really wanting to know what she was talking about.

"A gas will be released that will slow those things down. If we breathe it, it'll kill us; it only wears them down. Temporarily."

She pulled on her mask and motioned for him to do the same. Griffin put on the mask, but it took some getting used to.

"Stay close behind me and watch my six."

She opened the door and the room began filling with a thick fog. He slowly moved out and followed her closely. He walked carefully with his back to hers.

"What about the guy in the security room?" Griffin asked.

"The SR is isolated. As long as he doesn't open that door, he's safe."

She rounded the corner and aimed her gun. The room was empty but a faint glow could be seen in the far wall.

"Shit," she said, aiming her flashlight at the glowing.

"He opened the door?"

"The door was opened from the outside."

She aimed her gun into the security room then lowered it when she finished her sweep. He walked in and looked around. The screens were splattered in blood. The man hung from a thick yellow substance. He was split open starting at his neck down to his waist.

"Those little things did this?" He asked, amazed.

"No. I have never seen this before."

The man moaned and blood squirted from the wound as a tentacle shot out at Griffin's head. He dodged out of the way as it smacked into the wall behind him.

"Move," Jill said, dodging another tentacle.

She rolled across the floor and got onto her knees and fired at the man. The tentacles were about as big around as an arm and the ends were mouths. Each circular mouth lined with tiny teeth, serrated and curved back. Griffin dodged another and rolled out into the hall as Jill fired several more times at the hanging man.

"We're dealing with something new," she said, out of breath as the hanging man kept moaning.

There was banging coming from the vents above them like something running then an eerie giggling noise. Griffin aimed his gun up, but Jill grabbed it and mouthed the word "don't'. There was a shriek then it ran off further into the building. He sighed in relief.

"It sounded like a child," Jill said, after a moment. "All the children died during our first winter."

"I guess they're back," Griffin tried.

"What do you know about the Necrophagous virus?" She asked him.

"It's a hard word to say."

"It's reanimating their bodies."

"Like zombies?"

"No. They're not mindless flesh eaters. These things are smart. They hunt. These things are like wolves."

They left the main building and headed for the safe house. The trudge through the snow wasn't too bad. The wind had calmed and the snow was falling in steady sheets. As they rounded the fence, there was a gunshot. Another. Jill started to run but Griffin grabbed her.

"Don't be so quick," he put two fingers to his eyes then pointed to a large mound of snow.

Carefully, they climbed the mound and peered over. There were several more gunshots. What they saw was a horrific scene. The snow was littered with torn apart bodies. Large shapes could be seen rushing towards the house as more gunshots echoed.

"We're too late," she said.

He could tell she was on the verge of tears. Looking back at the building, and then to the house and the carnage going on before them. Screwed. Stuck in the middle with nowhere to go. They wouldn't survive out here very long. The cold would kill them or the creatures would find them.

"We have to do something. We can't just stay here."

"The dog shed."

She grabbed his hand and made a run for the shed. It was twenty feet to the right, an easy run. They reached the door when a loud screech surfaced. Griffin turned around to see three shapes running towards them.

"This isn't going to work. They have seen us," he said, raising his gun.

He held the trigger and the gun gave a burst. Though his first time firing a gun, it was only normal that every one of the bullets missed the target. He aimed again.

"Hold the gun steady. You control it not the other way around. I have to get this door open. There are explosives in here."

She kept fumbling with the lock as Griffin fired again, this time not as bad as the first. Several bullets hit the creature on the left. It fell and rolled down the snow embankment. Griffin aimed for the next one. Fired. It fell and didn't get back up.

"I've about got it," she said.

"No rush." He said, firing at the last one.

It fell and rolled down the slope towards them. It was small and thin. It had to be one of the children Jill was talking about earlier. Its flesh was grey with a bluish tint. It was naked aside from a cloth wrapped around it like a diaper.

Jill turned around to look at the creature dying at their feet.

"We need to plant the explosives in the main building," she said, unable to look away from the creature.

It jerked as 'its thick blood oozed out onto the snow. Dried black blood had hardened in the corners of its mouth which were lined with double rows of jagged teeth. Its hands consisted of three fingers with six-inch talons on each one.

"Put it out of its misery," Jill said, walking back to the door.

Griffin aimed the gun at the creature's head and hesitated. It lifted 'its head and moved its mouth as if to speak then fell back dead. He shot one time through the center of the forehead just to be sure. He followed her into the shed. It wasn't very big. It was sectioned off with chain link fence down the center. On the left side was storage and the right side was where the dogs were kept. Griffin looked over at where the dogs were supposed to be.

"Where are the dogs?" He asked, as she grabbed a bag off the top shelf.

She looked back over at him and then the dog pen. There were several holes, perfectly round holes dug into the snow and ground.

"Dogs couldn't have dug those," Griffin said.

As soon as the words left his lips, the whole shack began to shake. The door was flung open and Ken grabbed the back of Griffin's coat and jerked him back.

"Get out of there!"

Jill ran for the door as Griffin was pulled back by Ken. She fell down beside him as the shed continued to shake. The east wall burst outward as a huge tentacle shot out. Then the west wall, then the whole shed collapsed and several more tentacles shot up into the sky towering ten feet into the air.

"We have to move," Ken said, pulling Griffin to his feet.

Jill jumped to her feet as they began running. There was a low growling then the whole place began to shake. Jill lost her footing and fell. Griffin ran back and pulled her back up. They had just begun running when the ground in front of them collapsed and the tentacles emerged. Each one opened at the end with four long black claws that opened like fingers.

Up came its head, next. Its long snout split into four sections revealing its gaping maw. A tentacle slammed down onto the snow between Jill and Griffin. Griffin rolled to the left and grabbed the bag. He jerked the bag open and grabbed one of the sticks of dynamite.

"Griffin!" Ken called from across the chasm.

He threw a round object to him but it fell short. Griffin dropped the bag and ran for the black ball. He jumped and rolled to the right as a tentacle slammed down. He jumped over another and grabbed the ball. Griffin turned around and started back but was stopped short as a tentacle swooped down at him catching him in the stomach and lifting him into the air.

The grenade fell into the snow below him. Jill dove for it, grabbed it then ran for the bag. She pulled the pin and dropped the grenade into the bag then tossed it at the creature. As planned, the monster swallowed it. Griffin held onto the slimy tentacle for dear life as it jerked back and forth. There was a boom then everything happened so fast it's just a blur. The tentacle he was on swung back then fell to the ground flinging him a hundred yards away.

Griffin landed on his back hard. It knocked the breath out of him and most likely broke a few ribs. He wheezed as he rolled over onto his stomach and pushed himself up onto his hands and knees to see chunks of the monster still falling. He sighed and pulled the gas mask off and wiped the sweat off his face with the scarf.

"Griffin!" Jill called as her and Ken ran over. "Are you okay."

"Never better. I could use a lot of alcohol though. Beer, anything."

Jill laughed and helped him to my feet. Ken socked him in the arm.

"That was either the bravest or stupidest thing I had ever seen. You got a death wish?"

"Stupid is my middle name," Griffin started to walk, but began to fall.

They both grabbed him and helped him stand. Griffin felt a sharp pain in the deepest part of his belly.

"Griffin?" Jill sounded far away. "Griffin?"

He felt drunk. His head was spinning and he couldn't stand up, his legs kept buckling under him. Griffin's body finally gave in and everything went black.

"We can use his infection to our advantage," the woman in the white lab coat said, as she drew blood from his arm.

"You think the two infections will counteract?" The man asked.

"No. In order to keep the virus in check, he'll need the basics of the Necrophagous. I hope he isn't a vegetarian. To keep his human side, we will insert this."

She held up a circular object about as big around as a baseball.

"This will be planted in his stomach. We'll be able to get

all the research data we need and keep him 'sane' using this," she explained.

Griffin woke with a start and sat up in bed. He was back inside the main building. The room was lighted from the window over the desk and the TV was on, but the volume turned off.

"Get that one. I think that's all of them," Jill said, from out in the hall.

He slid out of bed and pulled on his clothes which were folded neatly on the desk. Griffin opened the door and stepped out into the hall. Jill saw him and ran over and threw her arms around his neck.

"Are you okay?" She asked, kissing his cheek.

"I'm good. What are we doing in here? Those things…"

"It's okay. We took care of them."

Griffin followed her to the front door where Ken and a few other survivors were throwing bodies on the fire.

"What happened to me?" Griffin asked.

"You fainted."

"Do you know anything about a woman in a white lab coat?"

She shook her head and studied his eyes. She stared at them for a few moments longer before Griffin turned away.

"I can't say I do," she said.

Griffin walked out of the bathroom and over to the desk and picked up a piece of paper with Jill's writing on it. It was a letter thanking him for all he had done in the short time he had been here.

"What happened?" Jill asked from the doorway.

Griffin turned around to face her to see what she was talking about. She walked into the room and sat down on the bed.

"Those places on your back. What happened?"

He leaned back against the dresser and looked at her. She was pretty in her pink shirt and tan skirt. He crossed his arms over his bare chest and sighed.

"My father. When my mom died, he lost it. He takes his grief out on me. Those places are from a frying pan."

"My God," she said, taken aback.

"Pulled it right off the stove and whacked me in the shoulders with it. The first hit flung scorching hot grease." He pushed the towel wrapped around his waist down a little to show her his hip where he had another scar.

"Why didn't you get help?"

Griffin shook his head and walked over to the bed and sat down beside her.

"He's still my father."

She didn't say anything for a while then she touched his chest over his heart. Griffin looked over at her a little startled by her touch.

"There's a devil in here. It's fighting to get out. Don't let it."

He looked at her a little confused. She kissed him. Her lips were soft and warm.

"They did things to you. They dirtied your halo, but there's some good in you."

She pushed him back onto the bed and leaned over the top of him.

"There's something I love about you, Griffin."

Griffin was actually at a loss. *Should I be having the*

thoughts I was having knowing that Rachel was my girlfriend? He tried to object, but his body wouldn't let him. She rubbed her hands down his sides and untied the towel around his waist. She grabbed the blanket on the bed and pulled it over them. Her hips began moving against his.

Owen

Owen woke up lying on an exam table in what he perceived as a morgue. Danny and his friends had riddled his body with bullets and had sent his body into a temporary state of hibernation. He sat up and looked around; he was alone aside from a man on the other side of the room with his back towards him. Owen noticed a fuse box on the wall to his right; no sooner had he had the thought, one of his serpents materialized and smashed into it killing the power.

The man fumbled around and, eventually, found his flashlight and switched it on to see Owen standing in front of him. Owen grabbed the man by the neck, the man's flashlight throwing eerie light on his face then illuminating the serpent over his shoulder. The man barely got a scream out before the serpent tore his head from his shoulders. After allowing his serpents to feed for a few moments, Owen headed upstairs.

The overhead lights flashed on and off repeatedly, like something out of the horror movies Owen remembered watching as a kid, the kind of atmosphere where monsters waited to feast on your flesh. The only difference now was that he was the monster.

"Dad!" A voice called from further in the building.

The woman rounded the corner and before she could scream the serpents were on her. Owen watched emotionlessly as they tore the young woman apart. There was a part of his brain, the part that was still the real Owen, that was disgusted and mortified by the unspeakable acts he now found himself committing. This part of his brain fought for control, but was overpowered by the darkness taking over his body — these 'demons' that Oswald had put in him.

Owen moved into the shadows as he heard more voices and footsteps heading his way. His serpents left their prey and waited on the fresh meat.

"Oh my god!" A man's voice.

Then a scream from a woman. The serpents were eager to kill, they didn't waste any time. They shot from the darkness and brought hell to all that had found their way into their path. Owen stepped out and what he saw now really looked like one of his old horror movies; blood splattered walls, body parts torn free and slung all over the place and his 'demons' eating from the bodies.

The Owen part of his brain was sickened, the Owen Sheppard had made relished in the carnage as the demons feasted.

Nathan

Nathan pulled his hood tighter around his face, trying to conceal himself. He knew they were watching him; he could only run for so long. Eventually, they would catch him and kill him. In their eyes he was committing a crime, he was a rebel. Fraternizing with humans was against Blood code, humans were meals, blood bags, nothing more. Worse of all in their eyes, Nathan was in love with a human.

He had sworn he would protect her, he had tried but failed. Sam, the council's handyman hunted her down and drained her dry. Nathan wanted revenge but knew those actions would lead only to his own end. So, he settled for running. Hiding.

Thunder boomed overhead as Nathan walked down the sidewalk weaving through the bustle of people. Lightning lit up the world around him and he stopped dead in his tracks. The lightning revealed Sam standing at the end of the street, his maroon eyes blazing. The rain then started pouring down. People began running, heading for their homes, cars or shelter. Nathan acted before thinking.

He turned and ran back the way he came. Lightning flashed again revealing two more Bloods coming from that direction. Nathan bolted down an alley between two buildings and slid to a stop at the dead end. He turned around as the three vampires closed in. The glass windows on the sides of the shops cast their trashing reflections as they moved closer.

"Mr. Short. You're a tough guy to catch," Sam said, crossing his arms over his chest. "Running wasn't your best choice."

Nathan backed up pressing his back up against the wall as Sam moved closer.

"It's all part of the natural order; the weaker get picked off and killed while the strong conquer. A blood with a human," Sam made a disgusted noise. "We're better than that. We are next to God, and soon we will be God. Humans are pitiful insignificant beings put here for our food source and pleasure."

"So now you're going to kill me?" Nathan asked, feeling around behind him for any type of weapon.

"Kill you?" Sam laughed. "I have something so much sweeter in mind. Why kill you, when I can make you suffer."

That was when Sam made his move. Faster than Nathan could register, Sam was face to face with him. Sam punched Nathan in the chest, not with a fist but fingers pointed straight forward. Nathan felt Sam's fingers wrap around his heart. Nathan looked down as Sam pulled his hand slowly out of his chest. He watched as his beating heart thumped 'its last few beats.

"You never would drink human blood. Let's see how long that lasts now with no heart to process the dead blood."

Nathan dropped to his knees, the hole in his chest slowly healing until only a faint pink scar was left. Sam dropped the heart down in front of Nathan then turned and started walking away.

"Happy hunting."

Nathan stared at his heart lying out before him in the rain. Though the wound was gone, the pain still persisted, and hunger was starting to outweigh the pain.

Pain. Hunger. Pain. Hunger. Hunger. Hunger. HUNGER.

Nathan stumbled to his feet; everything around him seemed to be spinning. His head pounded. His eyes burning. He knew he was changing, but yet he continued to fight it. He didn't want to become one of them. He grabbed the wall to his right for support and grabbed his chest with his left hand. The scar was killing him with pain.

Nathan opened his mouth to yell in pain, but only a hoarse squeak came out and his canine teeth grew longer and sharper. He tried to scream again, nothing. All his teeth were sharp like daggers. He fell to his knees, he grabbed the tear in his shirt and ripped it open, his shoulders snapped. His groans becoming low growls as the skin on his elbows split and long black bony spike grew out of them. His skin took on a grayish tint.

Nathan stood up fully transformed and stuck his bat-like snout into the air, he could smell them. Hundreds of them. Millions. Lambs to the slaughter, an all you can eat buffet laid out before him. Nathan started for the street, the claws on his toes clicking with each step.

Lightning flashed illuminating his night vision and the prey he had his eyes set on. A group of five teenage girls. That was when the hunger took him, he was barely conscious of what was even happening. He swooped down on the group of girls and went in for the kill. He grabbed the first by the neck and snapped it. Spinning around, he caught the second in the stomach with the bone jutting from his left elbow. He grabbed the next by the hair and jerked her back and tore her jugular open. He kicked the next sending her into the wall with the force of being hit by a truck on the highway. The last he grabbed by the arm as she tried to run.

"Please... don't kill me," she pleaded.

Nathan cocked his head to the right looking at her. The terrified look on her face tore at him, he didn't want to kill her but he had no choice in the matter: the beast was free and it was hungry. Leathery wings burst from Nathan's back and wrapped around him and the girl. She screamed as Nathan tore into her neck.

Nathan sat in the shadows of a building staring at what was left of the five girls. For now, the hunger was satisfied, but for how long? How long before he was forced to kill again?

"You Nathan?"

Nathan looked up at the man standing across the alley. He looked like he was in his twenties with medium blonde hair and muscularly built. He looked like someone you didn't want to piss off.

"Your sister sent me. Kim," Michael took the picture out of his pocket and showed it to him. "She sent me to find you. Said you were in trouble."

"I can't go back. I can never go back. I'm a monster."

Michael knelt down in front of Nathan and looked at him.

"What we are doesn't makeup who we are. I'm not exactly human either. That's your handy work out there?"

Nathan shook his head.

"You know, I've spent ten years hunting down creatures like you and me. There's something different about you, I think you're a lot like me, and that's a good thing."

Michael stood up and held his hand down to Nathan. Nathan just stared up at him.

"Let me help you. I think, together, we can beat this thing."

Nathan took his hand and Michael pulled him up to his feet. Michael shrugged off his jacket and handed it to Nathan.

"Here. It'll cover up most of the blood on you."

"Thank you."

"No problem. So can I call you Nate?"

"Yeah."

"Okay, Nate. How'd you get all the way out here? It's a long way to walk."

"Four days nonstop. 2,600 miles."

Michael looked down at Nathan and laughed.

"That's crazy. I'm a lazy ass you won't catch me walking more than five miles. This is us."

Michael unlocked the doors to a black muscle car. Michael took Nathan by his makeshift home in an abandoned building on the far side of town to get his few belongings. Afterwards, they stopped at a motel for the night.

"Early start in the morning. Need to rest up. I'm going to shower," Michael said, going into the bathroom.

Nathan sat down on the foot of the bed closest to the wall and looked around. It was a lot different from his last home. He grabbed an acoustic guitar sitting across the room and sat back down on the bed and began strumming a few cords. He missed playing with his band back when he was

166

human. Back when things were normal.

He had used to play at school dances and restaurants back in his hometown. All of that was a distant memory now. He had been blooded during a home invasion. The attackers murdered his parents and took both him and his sister. Once at a safe spot, the attackers had raped and killed his sister.

He watched as they ripped her neck open then seemed to drink her blood. Now he knew that was exactly what they were doing. Once they had finished with her, they moved to him. Nathan hadn't pleaded for his life, there was too much anger built up inside of him. Anyone that knew him knew him as the shy timid boy, but now he wanted to make these men suffer.

He fought them every step of the way. Managed to draw blood from the one trying to hold him down, but all his struggles were in vain.

"You play?" Michael said, sitting down on the other bed drying his hair.

"I used to."

"Would it be too much if I asked you to play something?"

"I don't know. It's been a long time."

"It's okay if you don't want to."

Nathan sighed then began playing. The song wasn't easy for him to play, but it was one he felt like he needed to sing. It brought back so many memories of Kori, his late girlfriend.

"You're really good. Did you have a bad or something?"

"Yeah. I got blooded and everything went to hell from there. I lost my girlfriend, my friends, my family. All because some vampires broke into our house. The things they did to my sister... I swore I would hunt them all down and kill every last goddamn one of them."

Michael studied Nathan for a moment, seeing all the emotions behind his eyes. Something told Andrew that this kid needed his help; without it, he would surely get himself killed.

"If you really want to hunt them down, I can help you."

Shane dropped down onto the balcony outside Michael and Nathan's room. Quietly pulling the dagger from his hip holster, he jammed it between the door and the frame — a little push on the dagger and the lock popped out of its catch. Shane walked across the room and over to the few bags set beside the dresser.

He unzipped the first and rummaged through the contents. Nothing. He set that bag aside and picked up the next. He got the zipper halfway open when he felt the cold steel on the back of his neck.

"Who are you and what do you want?" Michael said.

Shane sighed and held his hands up while slowly standing up. Michael kept the gun pressed to the back of his neck the whole time.

"My name is Shane. I was just looking for food."

"Why?"

"I'm homeless. I don't have anything. You can check me; all I have is a knife."

Michael kept the gun on him with one hand while he patted the boy's pockets with his other.

"Turn around."

"What's going on?" Nathan asked, sitting up in bed.

"I swear that's all I was doing. I'll leave. Please..."

"Shut up."

Michael lowered the gun. Judging by the look of the kid he wasn't lying. His clothes were tattered and dirty, his face was covered in dried sweat and mud.

"A man told me to come up here. Louis," Shane said, still holding his hands up. "He said, you two would help me."

"Sorry, I'm not a charity, I can't help everyone," Michael said, sitting down on the edge of the bed. "You'll have to find help someplace else."

"Here."

Nathan tossed an apple over to Shane. Shane caught it and took a big bite. Michael pulled Nathan out onto the balcony while Shane devoured the apple.

"We can't afford to take in anyone else. I have to get you back safe."

"He's starved; we can't just shove him away. He'll die."

"By the looks of him, he doesn't have long anyway. He'd just slow us down."

Nathan looked back in the room at Shane chewing at the core of the apple. He knew he couldn't live with not helping this kid. He had to do something, even if the kid didn't make it.

"I can blood him."

"I won't let you do that. They're not all like you. They're not all like the vampires you have seen that you think are bad. Not everyone is cut out to be blooded, it goes bad sometimes."

"I have to try."

"Nathan!" Michael grabbed Nathan by the arm.

"I'm not going to let him die if I can save him."

Nathan turned to go back in, but stopped dead. A tall man was holding Shane blood pouring from two puncture wounds on his neck. The man looked up at them then disappeared. Shane dropped to the floor; Nathan ran over and pressed his hands over the bleeding wounds.

"Louis. You knew I wouldn't let the kid do it so you took care of it."

"You need him."

Michael spun around to see Louis standing beside him. Louis dropped a duffle bag at Michel's feet then clapped him on the shoulder.

"It may come in handy. Keep them both safe. Don't take Nathan back to his sister."

"Why not?"

"She is under his influence. You saving him was all part of a setup. The new kid has some useful skills you can use. Train them well."

"Wait. You're leaving me with two brats now?"

Louis vanished. Michael picked up the duffle bag and opened it, bags of blood.

"Michael, he's coming too."

Michael walked in and set the bag down and lifted Shane up and set him on the bed. Shane's head fell limply onto his chest and Michael popped him on the cheek a few times to bring him around. Shane looked around; his eyes a deep maroon color then they settled back to brown.

"What happened?" He asked.

"You're now a vampire," Michael said, sliding the duffle bag over in front of Shane. "When you get hungry."

"What is that?" Shane grabbed his stomach as it growled loudly.

Michael reached into the duffle bag and handed Shane a bag of blood. Shane looked disgusted at first then mesmerized. He bit into the bad and began sucking down the red gold, as vampires called it. He finished the first bag and grabbed another from the duffle bag. Michael and Nathan sat down on the other bed and watched.

"How many of those will he drink?" Nathan asked.

"All of them, most likely; you drained six people dry."

"I guess you only realize how animalistic it is when you're watching someone else. It's kind of gross."

"It's not like this every time. The initial hunger is the worst. You literally drink until you can't anymore; after that, you only take what you need to survive."

Shane finished the last bag then looked over at Nathan and Michael, blood all over his chin and down his neck.

"If you're staying, you're showering before you're getting into a bed," Michael said, leading Shane over to the bathroom. "You know how to use it?"

"I'm not stupid," Shane said, and closed the door.

Shane came out of the bathroom drying his hair with a towel as Michael and Nathan were packing up their stuff.

"Thank you, guys."

"Don't get too comfortable. I'm not a babysitter, we get back and I'm taking you to Louis."

"I can help you guys. I can carry my own."

"No! Look, kid, I appreciate what you are saying but the answer is no. If it'll make you feel like you've proven yourself, you can try and take down Nathan."

"I can take you down."

"Oh really?"

"Michael," Nathan said, giving him a stern look.

"He wants to go. We'll go."

Shane smiled as Michael popped his knuckles. Michael swung the first blow hitting Shane square in the nose. Shane stumbled back a few steps but didn't fall. He came at Michael with a left hook but missed; Michael punched Shane in the left ribs sending him to the floor.

"Michael, stop," Nathan said.

"You done, shrimp boat?"

Shane got back to his feet and raised his fists. Michael laughed and came at him. Shane dodged the first blow and managed to punch Michael in the chest, but was hit in the side of the head with what felt like a brick. Shane crumpled to the floor. Michael started back over to his bag then turned around to see Shane getting back up.

"You got spunk, kid. You just need to learn to stay down!" Michael put his foot on Shane's crotch and pushed sending him back into the wall.

Shane got back to his feet and stumbled towards Michael. His head was spinning. Throbbing. Everything was blurry and distorted. He shakily raised his fists.

"I'm tired of this now, kid."

"I won't give up."

Michael sighed then punched him as hard as he could knocking him out. Shane fell to the floor blood pooling from his mouth.

"What the hell, Michael?!" Nathan said, kneeling down beside Shane.

"He's a vampire. He'll recoup fast. Carry him out to the car, we need to get going."

Blake

JHM
Jane's hospital for the mental
Pittsburg, Pennsylvania
(First study of the supposed 'DEMON')
9:00 am

Blake sat staring at the wall as several doctors looked through the glass contemplating his condition. The small room contained only a small bed and a desk. Above the desk were three well-drawn pictures. The first was of a lighthouse and a beautiful ocean view; the second, a dense forest with deer. The third was a self-portrait. The door buzzed and a doctor entered. She unfolded her chair and sat down in front of Blake. She was dressed in her white coat and nurses' shoes. Her name tag read, 'Mary', and the syringes in her pocket showed she meant business.

"Hello, Blake. Are you going to talk to me today? You know I only want to help you. Can you tell me why you are here?"

Blake didn't move or speak. He remained absolutely still aside from the slight movement of breathing.

"I know how hard it is to lose someone. I lost my parents and I didn't have much luck growing up. I can help you."

Blake still said nothing.

"It says here that your parents died when you were nine. Do you want to talk about it?"

"Why don't you stay out of my life?" His voice was hoarse from lack of use.

The look on Blake's face let her know he was on the verge of breaking. She set her clipboard down to be ready in case he had another violent outburst. The one last week from another of her patients nearly cost her, her life. Blake was prone to violence, but he had never touched her. He would take his anger out on other objects around the room.

"I'm only here to help."

Blake moved and she reached for one of the syringes in her pocket. Blake pulled at the cuffs around his wrists then looked at her.

"You better get out. I can kill you with this chain."

Mary wasn't sure how to go about this situation. Blake had gotten pissed and broke things, but never had he threatened her. It was one of the reasons why she was hell-bent on working with him. He showed promise.

"Killing isn't the way to go. What has driven you to such anger?"

Blake stood up and reached forward. Mary used fluid movement and stuck the syringe into his stomach. Blake stumbled back laughing and fell onto the bed. He looked at her and smiled.

"Good girl. You're all going to die."

He lay back on the bed as sleep overtook him. Mary sighed and stood up. She walked over to the bed and pulled a band-aid out of her pocket. She pushed Blake's shirt up and placed the band-aid over the bleeding puncture wound. Blake had three other band-aids around his belly.

"He's a lost cause; it's time you realized that."

Mary turned around to see Mr. Jane standing in the doorway. She pulled Blake's shirt back down and walked over to him.

"I won't give up on him. I know that this isn't the real Blake. I'm determined to get the real Blake out," Mary said, handing Mr. Jane the empty syringe.

"Fourth one this week. Mary, the kid is a dead end. I don't know what you're thinking you can do for him but..."

"I can save him."

Mary pushed her way past him and headed for the front desk. Mr. Jane followed her.

"I'll give you one week. If there isn't any progress by then, he gets shipped out."

"Don't worry; I'll have him by mid-week."

"You better."

"I'm scared. There are people after me. Please help me." Blake sobbed holding his knees to his chest.

"Who's after you?" Mary asked.

"They want to kill me. I'm so scared."

Mary pulls Blake close. He continued to sob as a door slammed shut in the distance. Blake pulled away and looked around frantically.

"They're coming, we have to hide."

Mary sat up in bed, sweat beading down her face. She gasped and looked at the clock. She slid out of bed and went downstairs. She opened the fridge and poured a glass. She pulled the door shut and saw Blake. She jumped and dropped the glass which shattered —Blake was gone. She rubbed her eyes and sighed.

"Damn."

GIPRG
Government Issued Paranormal Research Group
Washington, DC
Monday — 7:00 am

The GIPRG building located beneath the state capital is the top-secret organization set up in the winter of '94. Specializing in capturing and servicing in the research of paranormal deformities. Bought out in the summer of '01 by Sheppard INC., it is now headed by Director Thomas Niles.

Niles walked down the red-carpeted hall towards the meeting hall. He was dressed in a blue suit and was carrying an armload of files. He lay out the folders specifically for a GIPRG agent. The folder to the right of Niles had the name 'BLAKE' written in bold black on the front. A soldier — from the US army —walked over to the table and picked up the folder marked Blake.

"Extract or expendable?"

"Sheppard wants him alive if possible. He believes he can turn him to our cause," Niles said, sliding envelope over to the soldier.

James's Hospital for the mental
Pittsburgh, Pennsylvania

Mary punched in her time card and started towards Blake's

room only to be stopped by Dr. Jane. He was dressed in his usual best. A black dress shirt and black dress pants freshly ironed and polished black shoes. He wore his white doctor's coat over this, but never buttoned the coat for that would cover his three hundred dollars custom made tie.

"Mary!" He called walking over with a folder tucked under his arm. She knew exactly what it was. "Can I speak to you for a moment?"

"I really need to check in on Blake first he…"

"It'll only take a moment."

Mary looked down the hall and sighed then walked over to Dr. Jane. Jane laid the folder out on the front desk and separated some papers. Mary tried to read bits of the writing, but he was moving through them too fast for her to read much. He flipped a pink paper over and Mary grabbed it.

"Jane, you're out of your mind," Mary said, reading the paper.

"I can't control the law, Mary. Linda pressed all the charges she could. She hired Robert Gardner to her case."

"Robert? You expect me to put this child on the stand to be ripped apart by the most feared lawyer in Pennsylvania?

"This is your case, Mary. You specifically asked for it. You have two days to get the kid a lawyer and be in court on Thursday."

Jane turned and left as Mary leaned on the desk and sighed. She looked at the bottom of the page where it had 'lethal injections' written in bold print. She put the papers back in the folder, and stuffed it into her bag heading for Blake's room. She unlocked the door and set her bag down beside the desk, and sat down across from Blake.

"They want to kill me," Blake said, never raising his

head. "Can't say I don't deserve it."

Mary looked at him a bit startled, racking her brain trying to figure out how he found out.

"How do you know that?"

"I can hear what you're thinking," Blake looked up at her; she could tell he wanted to breakdown in tears, but he was fighting it. "You're sitting there thinking this boy is the same age as my daughter and they want to execute him, but meanwhile you think about what I've done and that makes you unsure of me."

"I..."

"Don't lie to me! I'm tired of being lied to. I'm still a person and I..."

He stopped being able to fight back the tears any longer. Mary got up and sat down beside him; hesitantly, she wrapped an arm around him surprised he didn't pull away. She knew for sure that she was dealing with the real Blake today.

"It's going to be okay."

"No, it's not," He looked up at her, his eyes were puffy and red. "I'm so scared."

"I'm going to fight for you."

"Why do you try so hard? Why do you care so much?"

"Because I've been where you are. We have to go find you a lawyer. What do you say we stop for some lunch on the way?"

Blake looked down at his handcuffs then back up to Mary.

"Can we take these off?"

"No. You have to keep them on. I know they're uncomfortable."

Somewhere over the
South Atlantic

Mull lit a cigarette then leaned back in his seat and closed his eyes. He soon fell asleep and began dreaming the same dream that plagued him every time he closed his eyes. War is all he had known since he was sixteen. His father was a soldier, his grandfather was a soldier. It was up to him to keep the chain going.

Mull ran up behind a dumpster and crouched down as bullets tore over him. A building to his right shook from bombs a few hundred feet away. Mull ejected the magazine from his M-4 and slammed another in. He rose up and fired four well-placed shots taking out snipers in the windows ahead. He sprinted forward and slid behind a burning car. He rose up and hears a gunshot.

Mull awoke as the flight attendant lightly shook his shoulder. She was a nice-looking girl. Her blonde hair hung down a few inches past her shoulders and a small strand to the right was dyed pink. Her attendant uniform was tight fitting. Mull had no complaints there. She wore just the right amount of makeup; she was as beautiful as a hooker, but not trashy like one.

"Sir, you have a phone call in the attendant cabin," she said, with a voice sweet as honey. "If you'll follow me, please."

Mull stood up and followed the young girl to the front of the plane, and she handed him the phone.

"Mull, we have intel that they are putting the boy on trial. It wouldn't surprise me if that bitch of a doctor doesn't try everything in her power to protect him."

Jane's Hospital for the mental
Pittsburgh, Pennsylvania

"Wait here, Blake."

Mary walked over to the desk where the nurses were at their computer stations. She set her folder down and looked at Helen.

"I need the address for Mrs. James."

Blake watched as the two women conversed then looked down at the heavy metal handcuffs holding his wrists together, and the chain linking them to his ankle cuffs. He considered himself lucky not to be in an orange jumpsuit to go along with his chains. He couldn't help thinking he deserved worse than this. He was getting the first-class prisoner treatment because they thought he was a mental screw up. He looked over at the glass doors and imagined what it's like to be in the gentle breeze. To feel the sun on his face. The past three years, he'd been locked up in a small room and only allowed to go down the hall to the shower room. The sun was something he desperately missed, along with hot dogs and French fries.

He could die just to have them one day. Life was so much different here. There was no freedom, it was how he pictured living with Hitler would be. He was under dictation and he didn't really care for it. He could have been free. But He would've been a free monster, and a monster was something he never wanted to be.

"Okay, Blake, let's get going," Mary said, opening the glass doors.

Blake could hardly wait to feel the warmth, to breathe in the fresh air, to hear all the sounds of nature. He felt changed. A few days ago, he was a killer; today, he felt like he might actually be worth something. He stopped just outside the door and closed his eyes, and breathed in deeply — taking in all the scents and sounds of the world at once. His delicate ears rejoiced at the untamed world around them. He could hear so much.

He could hear the lawyer down the street talking about how his case was falling through. He could hear the hooker a few blocks away trying to get a ride with a burly man in a pickup.

"Blake?" Mary called.

Blake opened his eyes and looked at her.

"You ready?"

Blake followed her down the short flight of stairs and to her car in the parking lot behind the hospital. She unlocked the car and let him in. After helping him in, she started the car as Blake grabbed the dog tag hanging from the mirror.

"Believe and you will receive," Blake read. "Do you believe in me?"

"Of course I believe in you. You're sitting right beside me."

"I mean, do you believe that I can be human?"

"Blake, I believe this is the real you. This sweet innocent boy you are right now. That other Blake that is fighting to get out, you can't let him. You have to beat him. This is your body, not his."

"I don't like that Blake."

Mary took the dog tag off the mirror and put it around Blake's neck.

"There, maybe this will help. It'll remind you that good Blake is inside and that he is the real you. You believe in him and keep that bad Blake from coming back."

Blake looked down at the dog tag then back up to Mary.

"Thank you."

Blake watched out the window as the world passed by. The trees and grass a bright green under the beautiful blue sky. Mary rounded the corner to the diner on the intersection of Main and Wilcox. Blake felt his heart freeze. The neon letters atop the building read 'Stucky's Diner'. He looked over at Mary with fear and shock.

"Blake!" Lori yelled.

Blake fought against the two boys holding him down. His face was bloody from a busted lip and a black eye.

"Blake!!"

"Not here. Please."

"Try to forget about what happened. By coming here, maybe we can bring some closure to it."

"I can't go in there."

"Do I need to call Sara and tell her we are going somewhere else?"

"Who is Sara?" Blake asked, looking at her confused.

"My daughter. She's inside waiting on us with my step-son."

Blake looked at the diner and exhaled. Mary grabbed his hand and rubbed the top of it with her thumb.

"It's okay if you don't want to go in there. There's no problem going someplace else."

"Go get your daughter, we have to leave now!"

"What?"

"In exactly one minute, there is going to be a hired gun right there between the dumpster and the diner. He's going to shoot at me. It's going to hit me."

"Blake, you're talking nonsense."

Blake opened the door and got out. Mary turned the car off and got out after him.

"Blake, get back in the car. Bl…"

A gunshot stopped her and she ducked and covered her head. She looked up and over to where Blake had been standing.

"Blake!"

Mary ran to the other side of the car, and knelt down beside Blake. Blood gushed from his side. Onlookers in the diner watched on as the mercenary reloaded his rifle and walked towards them. Sara shoved her way past people to see.

"Mom!" Sara yelled running over to the car.

"Sara, get in the car. Ethan, help me get Blake in the back seat."

Ethan grabbed Blake under his arms and then slid him in. Mary jumped in and started the car as Ethan squeezed in the back with Blake — meanwhile, the mercenary pulled out a pistol and aimed at them. Mary slammed on the gas as bullets hit the trunk of the car. Before long, the mercenary was miles behind them. Mary looked in the mirror at Blake and Ethan.

"How is he?"

"He's bleeding all over the place."

"Put pressure on the wound."

Ethan pressed his hands over the hole in Blake's side. He

made a face as warm blood oozed between his fingers. Sara turned around to watch.

"Who is he?" Sara asked.

"His name is Blake. Just keep the pressure on the wound Ethan."

They traveled a bit further before Mary pulled over at a motel. Mary opened the back door and motioned for Ethan to climb out.

"He moved a second ago," Ethan said, pointing to the bloody handprint on the window.

"Go wipe that off," Mary said, handing him a piece of gauze. "Sara, can you help me get him inside?"

Sara threw one of Blake's arms around her shoulder and they took him into the motel room.

"Put him on this bed," Mary motioned for the one closest to the back.

Ethan came in and closed the door behind him and locked it. Mary ripped open a pack of gauze and ripped Blake's shirt open to reveal the wound. They all watched in amazement as the butt of the slug began protruding from the hole. It forced its way out as if someone were pulling it out. It fell onto the bed beside him. The hole slowly began to heal.

"What the hell was that?" Ethan said, breaking the silence.

"Okay guys, this is Blake. The Blake from the whole Stucky's Diner stuff."

"What?" Ethan asked, looking up from the room service menu.

"Hear me out. Blake here is a changed boy. I've been working with him for over a year now. You two are familiar with split personality disorder. That's Blake. The handcuffs stay on him at all times in case his other personality breaks free."

Mary took several syringes out of her pocket. Sara looked at the needles then to Blake.

"Have you had to stick him with those before?" Sara asked.

"Many times. But don't worry, Blake is fighting that personality, he's keeping control so far."

"I still don't trust him," Ethan said.

"Ethan, he is a person just like you and me. He's like you, he loves to draw."

"I'm nothing like that psych case."

Mary grabbed her purse and pulled out a sheet of drawing paper. She unfolded it and handed it to Sara. Sara looked at the drawing dumbfounded.

"I was going to ask him about this one, who does that look like?"

"It looks like me... and him. He's never seen me before. How..."

"I think there is a lot we don't know about Blake," Mary said, looking at the fresh skin where the gunshot wound had been.

Blake shifted on the bed; Mary grabbed the picture and shoved it back in her purse. She walked over and sat down on the edge of the bed.

"How do you feel?"

"Like I've been shot," Blake said, with a faint smile.

"How did you know about the gunman, and how did your wounds heal so quickly?"

Blake tried to sit up, but pain shot all through his body;

he tried again and managed to lean back against the wall.

"I just know things. I can see them before they happen. I can hear things. Thoughts."

"Well, this is Sara and Ethan."

"He hates me already," Blake said, looking over at Ethan.

Blake looked over at Sara and was drawn in by her deep brown eyes. Her blonde hair hanging down a little way past her shoulders and looking as smooth as silk. She stared back unable to pull her eyes away from him.

"Are you afraid of me?"

"No," she said, barely audible.

"Thank you."

"Blake," Mary said, grabbing her purse; she opened it and took out the drawing and unfolded it, handing it to Blake.

"You took one of my drawings?" Blake said, in an almost whine.

"Yes. I'm sorry. Can you tell me who this is?"

Mary pointed to the drawing that looked identical to Sara.

"I had a dream a few nights ago. So I drew it."

"What was your dream about, Blake?"

"That's me and Sara. In my dream, Sara and I were talking to you about…"

"About what Blake?" Mary asked, needing to know.

"I don't remember."

Blake looked down at the floor unable to make eye contact with any of them.

Mull pulled out his cell phone and put it to his ear. He thought over how to tell Niles he had jeopardized his mission. He got too trigger happy and shot the boy in the side, not in the head. Now, they were on the run. The fact that the trial will never happen now, the boy will be on the list of Americas' most wanted.

"Niles," Niles answered sounding half asleep.

"Sir, the boy is on the run."

"Stay on their trail," Mull reloaded his rifle as he listened to Niles give orders. "I'll have a team meet you in Georgia; we can't afford any more screw-ups."

"Understood."

Mull winced as memories flashed through his mind at those words — Tracking down a warlord in Somalia when a car bomb took out his entire squad. It left him alone. He caught up with the lord in a rundown hotel. He followed him up to the crumbling fifth floor. The outcome of that day left him with several mental scars. The warlord had grabbed a child and was using her as leverage. When Mull moved to apprehend him, the man just stepped back taking the child with him. Mull still had trouble sleeping at night remembering the look on that child's face.

Blake walked into the bathroom and stopped when he saw Sara sitting on the edge of the tub crying. She was gripping her cell phone tightly in her hands.

"Hi," Blake said, softly.

"Hey."

"What's wrong?"

"Stupid boyfriend broke up with me. He thinks I'm a psycho," Sara said, holding her arms out, palms up, to show Blake the scars down her arms. "He says these make me ugly

187

and he doesn't want to be seen with me."

"You were asking him to go to the prom with you," Blake said, walking over to a small radio sitting on the back of the toilet. "Will you dance with me?"

Blake turned on the radio and held his cuffed hands out to Sara. Sara hesitated for a moment, but took his hands.

"Sorry, I can't move all that good," Blake said, smiling at her. "Can I see your arms again?"

Sara held her arms out again, and Blake looked at them for a moment before putting his hand over the scars on her left arm, he closed his eyes. Sara watched him with curiosity as he flinched as if in pain a few times. He opened his eyes and looked at Sara.

"Can you hand me a towel?"

Sara noticed the blood dripping onto the floor from his arm.

"What happened?" Sara said, grabbing a towel, wrapping it around his arm.

She stopped and looked at his arm — confused.

"You're beautiful. Don't let anyone tell you you're not."

She pressed the towel firmly against the fresh cuts on his arm. Blake flinched.

"Get another towel, please."

She looked at his right arm as it was cut by an invisible blade. She grabbed another towel and wrapped it around the cuts, staring into his eyes as she pressed on the bleeding wounds.

"Don't."

"What?" Sara asked, a bit shocked.

"I know what you're thinking. An angel like you doesn't need to get mixed up with a devil like me."

"What if I don't give you a choice?"

"I'm not here for long. I'll have to leave, don't get attached."

"Leave?" She asked, confused.

"I only have so much time left. For what it's worth, I really like you," Blake turned and left as Sara racked her brain trying to take in all that had just happened.

Bruce

Now only two hours out of Tucson, Johnny had insisted they stop for a brief rest and to get prepared before the final stretch of their trip. Johnny had gone to get them some rooms while the others waited outside trying to draw as little attention as possible to themselves. Johnny returned with two keys and tossed Danny one.

"We got two rooms, two beds in each. How are we splitting up?"

"I'm not staying in a room with him," Bruce said, nodding towards Kyler.

"Bruce is with me; Johnny, you take Kyler."

"Let's simplify it. I'll take Kyler, Aramis, Logan, and Emma."

"Bruce, Tyler, Lee, and Megan with me," Danny said.

"Eight tomorrow we move out. Rest up."

They parted ways and went to their rooms to get some rest before their final push. After several hours, no one was able to sleep so Megan broke the silence.

"I'm gonna go check out the bar across the street. Anyone want to go with me?"

"I'll go," Danny said, getting up. "Ty?"

"Sure."

Danny, Megan, and Tyler left for the bar leaving Lee and Bruce in the room. Bruce got up off his pallet on the floor and sat on the foot of the bed that Lee wasn't on. Bruce dug his pack of smokes out of his bag and took one out.

"Mind if I smoke?"

"Only if you don't share," Lee said, getting up and sitting down on the foot of the bed beside Bruce.

Bruce lit the homemade cigarette then took a drag and passed it to Lee. Lee put it between his lips and took a deep breath in, exhaling slowly.

"It's been a long time since I last smoked. Soo hated it."

"Soo not in the picture anymore?"

"She's dead," Lee said, taking another drag.

"Sorry," Bruce said, taking the smoke back from Lee. "I had a boyfriend a while back that hated me smoking."

"You're gay?"

"I'm bi. If that offends you, like pretty much everyone else, I understand."

"Nah. I am too. Even if I wasn't, it wouldn't bother me."

"You and Danny are so cool. That Kyler guy was hassling me about it and Danny, just after getting patched up from having a cursed sword stabbed through him, chased me down and talked me into staying. He told me if anyone else gave me any trouble about it to let him know."

"Same here. I just met you, but I like you. Danny and I will take turns fucking up whoever gives you a hard time."

"Thanks."

"We got to have each other's backs, right? We demons get a bad rap even though we've never done anything to anyone."

"Yeah. I did trash a supermarket; Danny came and got

me out of lockup."

"Trashed a supermarket?" Lee said, with a laugh. "Didn't have the right cookies or something?"

"No. It was, again, someone bitching at me about my sexuality. Said they could tell from the way I carried myself and stood that I was a 'flamer'. I didn't hurt anybody. That's not me unless you hurt someone I care about. When that guy stabbed Danny, it was the second time I killed someone."

"The first?"

"The first time was by accident. I was out on my own, living on the street. I was ten, some guy tried to take what little I had. I was just trying to protect what was mine. I killed a man over a pack of crackers and an apple."

"Gotta do what we gotta do to survive."

"Thanks for being a friend. I've never had many."

"No problem, bud," Lee said, putting his arm around Bruce's shoulders.

Danny

Danny, Megan, and Tyler took a booth about midway inside the bar and enjoyed their drinks and snacks. Danny had to admit, the more he got to know Megan the more he liked her.

"So you are an archdemon?" Megan asked, after several minutes of silence between them.

"So I've been told."

"And you're an Envy demon?"

"Yep," Tyler said, through a mouthful of food.

"Those things. The snake things, they easy to control?"

"Far from it. They have minds of their own. I hear them talking up here," Danny tapped the side of his head. "In the beginning, it was like I blacked out when they came out. I would be there one minute and the next thing I knew there were bodies all around me and I had no idea where they came from."

"Sounds pretty scary. That they can control you."

"It was at first."

Tyler, bored with the conversation and seeing he had no part in it, got up and went to play around with one of the dart boards on the other side of the bar.

"What about you? What's your story?"

"Long and complicated."

"Sounds fun," Danny said, taking a sip from his bottle.

"Wanna go somewhere quieter to talk?"

Danny was confused for a moment. The only noise was the few people scattered about the bar and quiet music playing — then it set in what she actually meant.

"Yeah."

She got up and led him out of the bar and to the reception desk at the motel. She drew a wad of cash from her bag and rented them a room. Once they had the key, they made their way for the room. Once inside, Megan pulled her shirt off and wiggled out of her jeans. She then turned to Danny and pulled his shirt off of him and tossed it onto the floor, then unbuttoned his pants and he stepped out of them. They fell back onto the bed kissing and, eventually, worked their way into more intimate activities.

Mosiah

Mosiah made his way through the packed house; Ivan had thrown the party after they had won tonight's game. The entire football team was here along with what seemed like half the school. He finally navigated his way through the crowds and emerged out onto the porch. He took a deep breath of fresh air; he didn't really know what had been up with him today. Halfway through the game tonight, he had begun to feel light-headed, and now all this noise was making his head feel like it was about to explode. This wasn't him, he loved football and he loved the parties even more.

"You all right, Mo?"

"Yeah. Just needed some air."

"All right. Don't stay out here too long, all the action is inside."

Mosiah wiped sweat from his forehead and blinked several times trying to clear his vision as it went blurry. He felt like he was on fire, so he decided his best bet was to go chill in the pool. He walked around the side of Ivan's house and went into the backyard which was about as packed as the house. He got in the pool and sat down in a less crowded corner and just tried to relax.

"Having fun?" Jenny said, swimming over beside him.

"Yeah, It's great."

"I'm gonna get a beer, you want one?"

"I'm good. Thanks."

Mosiah felt a sharp pain in his back then heard a slosh then screams. He looked across the pool where the water was turning red. Mosiah quickly tried to climb out, but found that he couldn't make it very far before he felt a pulling feeling in his back. He fell back into the pool as two serpent-like heads emerged from the water and snatched two more victims and dragged them into the pool. Mosiah made another escape attempt, but was pulled back in by some invisible force attached to his back.

"Mosiah!" Jenny called over the screams and splashing.

"No! Go!" Mosiah yelled as he struggled to stay above the water.

No sooner had he uttered the words, one of the serpents grabbed Jenny and plunged her into the bloody water. Mosiah was pulled under and, as he fought to get back to the surface, he saw the four serpents seemed to lead back to him. Mosiah managed to get back to the surface and this time was able to climb out. He turned back to look at the pool, but couldn't see the creatures anywhere.

Mosiah ran for the house where people were still fighting to get out the front door. Mosiah pushed his way through the crowd just like everyone else was doing, and after making it past several people he heard screams from behind him. The serpents were now behind him tearing their way through the students. Mosiah dropped to his hands and knees; he could hear these things talking inside his head telling him to feast. He began to get pains in his stomach, he reached out and grabbed a boy running past him and pulled him down to the ground.

"Mosiah, what are you doing?" The boy choked out

looking terrified. "Mosiah!"

Mosiah in no control of his actions leaned down and bit into the boy's neck tearing free a large chunk of flesh.

Oswald pulled the SUV to a halt and stepped out followed by four other men in tactical gear and rifles. He had caught word of a demon attack and had managed to keep it quiet until they could investigate.

"I want it alive, non-lethal only."

Oswald and his team moved in slowly. From the front steps, they could already see the carnage inside. They moved into the house, stepping over bodies and parts of bodies. They could hear movement from the living room up to their right. Oswald slowly rounded the corner to see Mosiah on his knees holding an arm and tearing pieces of meat from it with his teeth. Mosiah looked up at Oswald then went back to eating.

"Mosiah, I'm Oswald Sheppard. This is probably all kind of scary for you right?"

Mosiah paid him little attention, he just kept eating. Oswald inched closer and squatted down. He didn't want to frighten the guy more than he already was and unlike Danny and Owen, he wasn't entirely sure what this guy was capable of. What limits did his powers hold?

"I can help you. I've helped many others like you. All this must seem so strange, but I can help you control it."

Oswald slowly extended his hand towards Mosiah. Mosiah stared at him for a moment before dropping the arm he had been eating from and took Oswald's hand.

"There we are. We're not going to hurt you. You'll be safe with us," Oswald explained as he led Mosiah out of the house and to the SUV.

Cody

Cody turned the shower off and wrapped his towel around his waist. He stopped at the mirror and looked at his reflection; he had had a rough night last night. He had been put on an assignment to find a cryptid causing all kinds of trouble on the edge of town. He had only got in a few hours ago, caught a few Zs then decided to clean up. He looked at the thin fading scars on his left side from a run in with a lycan a few years back, the mission that had very nearly been his last.

Cody and his brother, Quinn, had been born into this life of hunting cryptids; their father had started them early — by the time they were ten, they had each made their own kill. The thing was Cody didn't really want this life. Whereas Quinn had no issues with their line of work, Cody did. He realized that these things were just doing what they do to survive. He knew deep down that lycans and vampires still had some humanity within them. Which brought Cody to his next point, the lycan that had attacked him years ago, was now his lover.

She had brought him down with a slash to his side, but found herself unable to kill him, and he unable to kill her. They knew what they had was forbidden on both sides, she would be killed for loving a human and he would be killed for loving a lycan; though, technically, Cody was no longer human.

Cody dried off and pulled on his underwear and a pair of lounge pants. Cody walked out of the bathroom and up the hall and entered the kitchen. He grabbed a snack and a drink from the fridge then headed into the living room where Quinn was on the couch playing video games. He plopped down on the couch and opened his bag of chips and can of soda.

"You still do that weird shit?" Quinn asked, glancing over at Cody.

"I like my chips cold. Does it bother you that much?"

"It's not normal."

"And we're the picture of normal," Cody said, shoving some chips in his mouth. "If you think we're normal then you got problems."

"Everyone has a different view of what they see as normal," Quinn explained never looking away from the TV where he was gunning some other players down. "So I guess we're just as normal as everyone else."

"Nice way to sum it up," Cody said, taking a drink from his can.

"Can't help it I'm the smart one. Wasn't it you that thought when I was talking about a cajin chupacabra you thought I was talking about some new kind of fried chicken?"

"Shut up."

"Wanna run and pick up some cajun chupacabra?"

Cody looked over at Quinn and burped.

"Nice. Smells like you ate some rotten chupacabra."

"Let me see it," Cody said, snatching the controller from Quinn.

"Dude! You're gonna kill me."

"You're sucking, let me help you out."

"No. Last time you tried to help me out, you managed somehow — it still boggles my fuckin' mind — to wipe my consoles entire hard-drive." Quinn managed to snatch the controller back. "This is like sacred to me. This is my ark of the covenant, you don't touch it."

"You died," Cody said, pointing to the TV.

Quinn looked back at the screen and sighed.

"I was this close to setting a new record," Quinn said, holding his fingers an inch apart.

"Record for what? Nerding out for twenty-four hours straight?"

"You'll never understand me."

"I don't think any would."

"If you weren't my brother, I'd hit you right now."

"You couldn't land a hit if you tried."

"That a challenge?"

Cody got up and walked over to a large open section of the living room followed by Quinn. If there was one thing these two loved more than each other it was competition. Cody figured a way to make this more interesting would be to place a bet on it but as he reached for his wallet, he remembered he was in his lounge pants.

"Fifty bucks says you can't land a single hit on me," Cody said.

"Deal," Quinn said, and lunged for Cody.

Cody easily dodged Quinn's blows and tripped him sending him onto his back.

"Gotta be faster than that little brother."

Quinn jumped to his feet and got ready for another go.

Quinn attacked again, this time aiming low then with a surprise high swing which Cody barely dodged. Quinn kept the pressure on, mixing up his fighting styles trying to confuse Cody. The only downfall for Quinn was that Cody had taught him everything he knew about fighting so Cody knew all his moves. Cody dodged a barrage of swings then put Quinn in a headlock and wrestled him down onto the floor where he pinned him down.

"You're getting better, but you still can't take me down."

"What the fuck are you two doing?"

They both looked up to see Lewis standing in the doorway.

"Practicing," Cody said, standing up.

"Kicking your brother's ass is more of what it looked like."

"We had a bet. Fifty said, he couldn't land a hit on me."

"Did he?"

"No," Quinn said.

"I'll triple it if either one of you can hit me."

"Sir?"

Lewis dropped his bag on the kitchen table and took a few steps forward and spread his arms out. Cody looked over at Quinn and shook his head, but Quinn wasn't about to turn down a challenge or a chance at some cash. Quinn ran full force for Lewis who quickly sidestepped to dodge Quinn's blow then grabbed Quinn by the back of the neck and shoved him to the floor.

"I told you not to," Cody said, crossing his arms over his chest.

"I'll quadruple the wager. Want to go again?" Lewis asked, as Quinn got to his feet.

Quinn went into full-on attack mode trying with every part of his being to land a hit on Lewis and rake in that cash but to no avail, Lewis laid him out each and every time. With each failure, Lewis would up the reward, and each time Quinn would fail.

"I fear you both are missing the point of this exercise," Lewis said, shoving Quinn to the ground for what seemed like the hundredth time. "You both are great hunters, powerful on your own. But if you worked together, you could be nearly unstoppable."

Quinn and Cody both looked at each other and without words; they knew exactly what the other was thinking. They both set themselves upon Lewis. Lewis managed easily to dodge and block all their attacks. Lewis tripped Quinn and grabbed Cody by the arm and flipped him slamming him down onto his back. Cody gasped trying to catch his breath as Quinn got to his feet.

"You're both fighting me, yet you're not working together. Until you two learn to be in sync with each other you'll never be able to move up in the hunter world," Lewis said, walking over to the table where he had dropped his bag. "I expect dinner will be ready by six and the dishes washed and put away by seven."

"Yes, sir." Cody and Quinn both said.

Quinn offered Cody a hand then pulled him to his feet and they headed into the kitchen where they began to prepare dinner. They found themselves doing this more and more often as they failed Lewis' tests, some of them seeming more and more ridiculous.

"You think he'd notice if I slipped some shit into his food? The neighbor's dog lays these massive shits, we just..."

Quinn imitated scooping some up then dropping it into the pot on the stove.

"You want more chores, don't you? He may act like an ass, but where would we be without him? Back out on the street again like after...like after mom and dad," Cody said, regretting bringing up their parents. "The water boiling yet?"

"Yea."

"Sorry I brought it up. I wasn't thinking."

"It's okay," Quinn said, pouring the noodles into the pot.

"Hey," Cody said, grabbing Quinn's shoulder. "You know I'll never let anything like that happen to you."

Quinn nodded stirring the pot of pasta.

"I mean it. I'll die before I let anyone hurt you."

"Lewis kind of hurt my neck when he grabbed me and slammed me down."

"Hurt hurt, spaz," Cody said, socking Quinn in the arm.

Owen

Owen used his old lock picking knowledge to unlock the motel room door and went inside. He stripped off his bloodstained clothes and got in the shower. He stood under the hot water just letting it wash over him, washing away the stress and fear he felt. For now, he was alone, himself. The other Owen was nowhere to be found and his demons sated by their meal. Owen would do anything to rid himself of his 'other personality' and the darkness dwelling within him.

He had killed so many since Sheppard had released him, but one encounter had stuck with him. The guy Sheppard had ordered him to bring back. When fighting him, Owen had felt something different. An almost feeling of hope before the other Owen took over and the real Owen was left as a silent observer. Something about this Danny guy had given him the hope that he could be brought back to his former self, he just didn't know how.

Owen got out of the shower and dried off then got dressed in some clothes out of a suitcase he swiped from a car in the parking lot. He lay down on the bed lost in his thoughts. He would find a way to rid himself of this other side and get back to the person he wanted to be if it was the last thing he did. Fuck Sheppard and whatever his plans were, he could find a way to contact this Danny and plead for his help, he just hoped he could keep his darkness locked away long enough to do so.

Mosiah

Mosiah wasn't sure what he had gotten himself involved in. He now found himself in some lab deep beneath Tucson and frankly, some of the things he had seen in his short time here, scared the shit out of him. Sheppard had taken him to his room and left him to get settled in. He had showered and changed out of his blood-soaked clothes into some fresh clothes he had found in the closet. He sat down on the foot of the bed facing the mirrored door closet.

He stared at himself, wondering what he had become. He wiped at some dried blood in the corner of his mouth he had missed. He was only semi-aware of what had happened at the party, he remembered those things coming out of him. Those things slaughtering all his friends, as he was helplessly bent to their will. His brain didn't want to believe any of it, he wanted it all to be some horrid nightmare to be left in the past. He looked away from his reflection as the door opened.

"Would you allow us to run a few tests, just to get a feel for how far along you are in the process?" Oswald asked, leaning against the doorframe.

"There's more?"

Without some bloodwork, I can't tell you at what point in the gestation you are."

"Yeah." Mosiah said, standing up and following Oswald.

"These tests are painless, I promise. We'll just draw a little blood; get a swab of your throat, and a urine sample."

"You said, you helped more like me. What am I?"

"You, my son, are the next step in evolution."

Sheppard waved his ID over a small box on the wall and a set of doors opened up to reveal a lab where several people in lab coats were busy with their work. Oswald led Mosiah over to a chair and had him sit down. As soon as he sat down, a girl walked over with her hands full of supplies.

"Okay, Mosiah, the first thing we're going to do is draw some blood," she stretched his arm out and began feeling for a vein. "Make a fist for me."

Once satisfied she had found a vein, she stuck the needle into his arm then attached one of the vials and it instantly began to fill with blood.

"You all right?" She asked, as she connected the fourth vial.

"Great," he said, though he wasn't sure she heard him as low as it came out.

"All done with that part," she said, pulling the needle from his arm and placing a bandage over the area. "Tilt your head back a little and stick your tongue out."

Mosiah followed her directions and she jabbed, what looked like to Mosiah, the longest Q tip down his throat. After nearly gagging him to death, she handed him a cup.

"Bathroom?" Mosiah asked.

"We need you to do it here. No contaminants."

"In front of all these people?"

"Yours isn't the first penis we have seen, nor will it be the last."

After several minutes of trying to imagine he was alone in the room, he was finally able to give them a urine sample. Once done with all the testing, Sheppard led Mosiah out into the hall.

"Sorry if that was a bit embarrassing for you. They are funny about their tests."

Mosiah nodded, not really knowing what to say. He honestly just wanted to go back to his room and curl up in the bed and try to forget the past twenty-four hours.

"You hungry? You should really get a bite to eat after giving that much blood. Let me show you to the mess hall."

Owen

Owen was woken by the phone Sheppard had given him going off in his pocket. He rolled over and pulled it out and looked at the screen, a message from Sheppard. Owen red over it twice making sure he hadn't misread still being half asleep. Sheppard was telling him there had been a change in their plans, Danny was no longer the priority and that he was to meet with someone named Kenyon to receive his next instructions.

Owen got up and gathered his things and headed for the address at the bottom of the text. Ten minutes later, he found himself facing a rundown looking apartment building. He went inside and climbed the stairs until he reached apartment 113. Owen raised his hand to knock, but before he could connect his knuckles to the door, it opened and he faced a man in his early thirties.

"Kenyon?"

"Come inside."

Owen stepped inside and Kenyon closed the door behind them. The inside of the apartment didn't look much different from the outside, rundown and like a squatter's hideout. Kenyon led Owen into a back room where there was a table covered with a sheet and what appeared to be a body underneath it.

"Sheppard sent you here to pick this up."

"I was just told to come here for my next instructions, nothing about a body."

"This body is your next instruction. We have intel on where Danny and his group are held up. You are to take this body and wait for Tyler to separate from the group. Once you have Tyler alone," Kenyon tossed Owen a brown bottle. "Chloroform him and bring him back here. But before you leave, you're to use this body to make the scene look like you slaughtered him."

"I thought from Sheppard's text Danny was no longer the priority?"

"I just get orders from the big man. I don't ask questions."

Kenyon pulled the sheet back to reveal the body laid out on the table which shared a striking resemblance to Tyler.

"How did you find someone who looks nearly identical?" Owen asked, looking at the face of the body.

"It's what I do. You have a lot of work to do, you best be hitting the road."

"And I'm just supposed to walk out of here carrying a body?"

"Beauties of living in this area. There's a car downstairs for you. Good luck rookie."

Danny

Danny lay on the bed fast asleep as Megan lay beside him. She reached over and brushed some hair out of his face. She hadn't been one to believe in love at first sight, but that all changed when she first laid eyes on Danny. Something about him felt right, like fate had brought them together for a reason. She slid over closer to him and laid her head on his chest and put a hand on his stomach and rubbed around his bellybutton.

"Can't sleep?"

"Sorry, I didn't mean to wake you. I just wanted to play with your belly button, it's so cute."

"I don't mind," Danny said, wrapping his arms around her.

"Can I ask you something?"

"Sure."

"Is this a no strings attached, one-time fling for you?"

"I don't want it to be. You?" Danny answered.

"No. I've fallen for you, Danny Carter," she said, then kissed him.

"You just like me for my body," Danny joked.

"Oh, yeah. Your face is blech, but your body is a ten," she laughed.

"I just like you for your amazing jugs."

Danny laughed then kissed her several times, he had to admit he hadn't felt this good in a long time. He had been so afraid to commit to someone after his last love, but things felt different with Megan.

"Should we get back to the others?" She asked.

"We should, but why ruin what we have here? They are all big guys; they can handle themselves for a few more hours."

"What are you saying?" She said, with a smile.

"Round two?" Danny said, arching his eyebrow.

Tyler returned to the room and quietly went into the bathroom to change and get ready to hit the hay. He splashed some water onto his face as the window to his right burst open and he was slammed back against the door. Tyler instantly recognized the guy as the one they had faced off against earlier: the one who had killed Aramis' best friend.

Owen pressed a cloth over Tyler's mouth and nose, forcing him to breathe in the chemical he had soaked the cloth in. Tyler fought for a few moments before he felt his body losing its strength and sleep overtaking him. Once Owen was sure Tyler was out, he climbed back out the window with Tyler and leaned him up against the wall and then picked up the body he had been given to fake Tyler's death.

Owen climbed back through the window and then set about tearing the body to pieces, making enough noise to be sure to get the attention of the others out in the room. Once he heard someone rattle the door handle, he climbed back out and picked up Tyler, leaving the scene.

The Prophet

Harrison stood at the pulpit staring out at the empty church. He never failed to see the beauty of his religious establishment, even when the sanctuary was empty. A door to Harrison's left opened and Lucas entered with a sheet of paper which he quickly brought to Harrison.

"A fax, sir."

"Thank you, brother," Harrison said, taking the paper and glancing over it. "Lucas, would you be so kind as to put the word out that we need a prayer meeting this evening."

"Right away, sir," Lucas said, and started away.

"And Lucas, find Landon. Whatever sinful activities he is occupied in today will have to wait. It's time."

Lucas nodded before taking his leave. Harrison took a deep breath in and slowly let it out. He knew this day was coming and all he could do was try and have his flock ready. He hoped he had taught them well enough, and prepared them for the Day of Judgment, even his rambunctious and rebel son. Harrison walked down the three stairs and knelt down facing the pulpit and the large crucifix behind it and prayed.

Landon rounded the final turn with a good headway on the

other racers. He cleared the turn then gunned the throttle, zooming forward towards the finish line. Landon glanced back over his shoulder as Christian gained on him. Landon twisted the throttle again only to have his chain break, the sudden break causing him to lose focus and lose control of the bike. Landon rolled off the bike before it began somersaulting further down the track, he rolled to a stop and sat up as his bike came to a stop several hundred feet away.

Landon sighed pulling his helmet off. He got up and began his walk of shame to his bike as the other racers zoomed past him to secure their places in the running. He got to his bike and stood it up and began walking it back to the pit. He silently cursed realizing the toll the crash had taken on his bike, not only did he have a broken chain, but he also now had a bent front wheel and his finder had broken.

He rolled his bike over to his team and tossed his helmet to the ground in frustration. His team, or should he say his friends, were there to check on him after his crash and make sure he was okay but he wasn't in the mood to socialize.

"You okay?" Kate asked him.

Kate was the only other person he knew who loved racing as much as he did, and they had instantly hit it off when she had moved to town; two months later, and they were not only best friends but dating.

"I'm fine, my pride's not," Landon said, pulling his shirt off and tossing it into the backseat of the truck. "That's it for me this go round."

"We'll get the next one."

"If we can afford to repair the bike," Landon said, grabbing a drink from their cooler and cracking it open. "We tapped out with the last repairs."

"Kate! Need a hand over here," Sawyer called from over at the bike.

"We'll figure it out," she said, socking him in the shoulder before heading over to help with the bike.

Landon sighed and sat down on the cooler and took a chug from his drink. He was beginning to lose faith in himself, that he had what it took to become a professional racer. He had had his hot streak but here lately he was having problem after problem and couldn't afford to fix them. He felt lucky though, these five people, his team, they all believed in him and always persuaded him to keep at it.

"Tough break, Bird," Christian said, walking over followed by his team. "Maybe next time you buy a bike that is worth more than 'its weight in shit."

Landon got up and started over to his team and bike.

"See, he's too much of a pussy to even throw out a comeback," Christian laughed. "Good thing you got that girl on your team. She's got more balls than you, Bird. I might have to get in her."

That was when Landon lost it. He had dealt with enough of Christian's shit for far too long. Landon ran and tackled Christian and began punching him. It wasn't long before Christian overpowered him and slung him off. Christian was a big muscular guy, nearly double Landon's size. Kate looked up as several people went running by and turned to look back at the commotion.

"Shit," Kate said, running over and grabbed Landon, trying to pull him away. "Landon, stop!"

Landon got control of himself and after giving Christian the evilest look he could, and turned and headed back for the truck.

"We're not done, Bird! You're lucky your girlfriend saved your ass!"

Landon sat back down on the cooler and was instantly surrounded by Ethan and Tony. Ethan handed him a clean rag to clean himself up, his lip was busted and his nose was bleeding along with a soon to be black eye.

"It's been a shitty day man," Tony said, patting Landon's shoulder.

"What the hell was that?" Kate asked, walking over. "Are you trying to get kick out where you can't race anymore?"

"I lost my shit. Sorry."

Landon picked up his can of drink so Kate could sit down beside him.

"Whatever that asshole says, you can't let it get to you. He's trying to get you kicked out, he's afraid of you. You're the only real competition he has out here."

"Yeah. Sure looks like it," Landon said, looking over at his bike then took a chug of his energy drink.

"We've got this. It may not be this year, but you'll get the win."

"Maybe," Landon said.

"We're not giving up on you," Kate said, grabbing his chin and turning his head to face her. "Me, Ethan and Tony, we love you and are going to see you through to the end."

"Thanks. Let's get the bike packed up so we can go work on it."

Landon and Kate walked over to help Ethan and Tony load up the bike and their supplies.

"Landon!"

Landon turned to see Lucas walking over and silently

cursed. They finished securing the bike in the back of the truck and Landon grabbed a clean shirt from the backseat as Lucas walked up.

"Your father is in need of you."

"What now?" Landon asked, pulling on his shirt.

"He's called an emergency prayer meeting and needs you in attendance."

"Meet up with you guys tomorrow I guess," Landon said, turning back to his team.

Landon walked over to Kate and pulled her into a hug.

"Love you."

"Love you too," He said, then kissed her. "See you tomorrow."

Danny

Danny lay back onto his back breathing heavily. Megan rolled over, resting her head on his chest — she rubbed his smooth chest.

"I think you hold the record," she said, playing with his nipple.

"What was the previous?"

"Twice."

"Shit, we doubled that."

"That we did. Surprised we haven't been interrupted by anyone since we left."

"Don't jinx it. Let's savor this moment of happiness before we're thrust into the shit again."

An insistent knocking rattled the door, causing both of them to jump.

"We just got flushed."

Danny laughed then kissed her before sitting up and pulling on his underwear. He walked over to his clothes and pulled on his pants. The knocking came again. Danny opened the door to be greeted by Johnny, who looked like he had just seen a ghost.

"Tyler..."

That was all it took to snap Danny from his momentary

paradise. Danny grabbed the leather jacket Emma had given him and rushed past Johnny pulling the jacket on over his bare torso as he went. Danny took the stairs two at a time and as he reached the bottom a heavy rain had started and standing in the middle of the parking lot was Owen.

"What have you done to Tyler?"

"Danny!" Johnny called coming up behind him. "He killed Tyler."

Lightning flashed and Owen could see the demon hiding behind Danny's eyes, the darkness he had hidden deep within himself forcing its way to the surface, and he knew he was the one that it was coming for.

"Danny, listen to me..."

Danny thrust his hand forward and his left serpent shot forward. Owen had never seen it materialize. He dropped and rolled to the side as the serpent struck the pavement where he had just stood. Danny thrust his right hand forward and the other serpent shot forward nearly catching Owen's arm as he rolled out of the way again.

"Danny, Listen!" Owen called over the pouring rain and crashing thunder. "I didn't kill your brother!"

Lightning flashed again and Owen noticed a change coming over Danny. The darkness seemed to be covering him, and that kindness he had wanted to find in this savior was gone, replaced by the demon that also called Danny's body home. Megan emerged from the room and leaned on the railing looking down on the fight below; even she noticed something different about Danny.

"Danny!" Owen called.

Danny looked up at him with eyes red as blood and his teeth becoming sharp like tiny daggers. His flesh began taking on a grayish tint, his veins standing out against the pale flesh.

"Danny," Johnny said, placing a hand on Danny's shoulder.

Danny turned with lightning fast speed and grabbed Johnny by the neck and slammed him back against the wall.

"Danny, stop," Johnny choked out as Danny's grip tightened.

Owen noticed that Danny's serpents had disappeared, the darkness taking full control of his body, not fighting alongside it. Owen willed his own serpents and shot them forward, each one biting into Danny's shoulders. The pain of the bite caused Danny to drop Johnny, his attention going back to Owen.

"Your brother is alive! Stop this!"

Owen could tell he wasn't getting through. Whatever Sheppard had done to him, it was clearly far beyond what had been done to himself and now it was showing 'its full force. Owen knew his strength and he knew that whatever Danny was becoming he had no chance against, his only hope was to somehow get through to him.

"Sheppard has Tyler!"

Danny charged him, tearing free of the serpents and tackling Owen. Danny straddled him, opening his mouth revealing the needlepoints of his teeth before biting into Owen's shoulder. Danny pulled away tearing a hunk of flesh and cloth from Owen's shoulder. Danny spit out the flesh he had torn free and looked down at Owen as he licked the blood from his lips.

"Danny, stop."

Danny was about to go for another bit when he felt

Megan wrap her arms around him. She could feel his heart beating like it was on the outside of his chest. She wrapped him tighter as Owen slid out from under him and got to his knees, a hand placed firmly over the gushing wound on his shoulder. Megan laid her head against his back.

"This isn't you. Come back to me, Danny. Come back."

She could feel him fighting to regain control of his body, trying to get the darkness back under control. She didn't know if what she was about to say was a lie or not, but she had to get him back before he became too far gone to come back.

"Tyler is alive. Come back to me so we can go save him."

She let go long enough to get around in front of him, she gently wiped his face off with her sleeve.

"I love you, Danny. Come back to me," she said, then kissed him.

She noticed the color of his skin returning to normal, slowly but surely. His eyes losing their red shade and returning to their normal brown. She wrapped him in her arms and held him as tight as she could until she felt his body relax and slump against her. She looked over at his head lying on her shoulder; he had passed out exerting himself in the fight to gain control of his body once more. Megan looked over at Johnny and nodded to him.

Johnny walked over rubbing his bruised neck and looked over at Owen as the wound in his shoulder slowly healed.

"Do we trust him?"

"I don't know. Why kill Tyler, and then hang around to tell Danny he didn't?" Johnny said. "Then again, he could be telling the truth. Fake killing Tyler to play Danny right into

Sheppard's hands."

"Let's get him inside," she said, gently laying Danny down so she could grab his feet and Johnny his arms.

"I stayed... because I'm done with Sheppard. Tyler is alive."

Johnny looked at Megan for her thoughts.

"Follow us. But if you try anything..."

"I won't."

They laid Danny on the bed and Megan set about stripping him down and drying him off and redressing him. She covered him with the blankets while Johnny cleaned Owen's wound with peroxide and bandaged it. The wound was healing, but much slower than usual.

"They had me take Tyler and then leave the look alike they found to make Danny believe I had killed his brother. To force Danny's hand."

"Danny doesn't even know Tyler is his brother."

"He knows. Deep down, Sheppard may have wiped a lot of his memories but the bond they had, Sheppard couldn't touch. He knew if Danny thought Tyler was dead, Danny would get reckless and expose himself. Knowing Sheppard, he probably contacted the Prophet."

"The Prophet?"

"A radical religious leader, who has it out for demons."

"Shit."

"Have Danny seen as a monster and the Prophet would make him out to be the antichrist here on earth, and anyone and everyone would be out to kill Danny."

"I thought he was hellbent on getting Danny?"

"Not anymore. He's found a new prodigy. Someone he believes is stronger, more controllable."

"And what is Sheppard's endgame? What is he trying to accomplish?"

"World dominance. He has a virus he's going to release to create a better world." Owen said, air quoting. "But in truth, it's hell on earth."

Megan walked over and leaned against the wall beside them.

"I know one thing. We can never let Danny reach that place again. Next time, he might not be able to come back. He's fought so hard to keep whatever Sheppard did to him locked away inside of him. He was terrified, I could see it in his eyes when I held him, he was afraid he wouldn't come back. I've only seen that type of fear once before, and it scares the hell out of me," she looked over at Danny on the bed. "He has a deep darkness in him, and as strong as Danny is, he's no match for it. My father was an arch-demon and this is exactly what destroyed him. Danny has been strong for us; he'd give his life for anyone of us. To help him defeat this darkness within him, are we prepared to give up ours for him?"

After a moment of silence, Bruce stepped forward.

"I will," Bruce answered.

"I will," Emma said, stepping forward.

"Aye," Logan said, stepping up beside Emma.

"Yes," Johnny said.

"If you'll have me, I will," Owen said, standing.

"Danny has my blade," Aramis said.

Everyone turned a bit stunned; these were the first words Aramis had spoken since Simon had been killed.

"And I," Megan said, looking over at Danny with a love she hadn't felt in a long time.

They all knew what it was they were agreeing to and they all meant their pledges. Danny, they knew, was most likely their only way of stopping the Sheppards. Of stopping the apocalypse they were teetering on the edge of. War was coming. They really had no power in stopping it, too many pieces were already in play.

Danny had a massive weight on his shoulders, hell they all did, he was the key piece in saving mankind and cryptids alike. A savior so to speak.